GW00363431

# NELL'S NOVEL

First published in 1999 by
Marino Books
an imprint of Mercier Press
16 Hume Street Dublin 2
Tel: (01) 661 5299; Fax: (01) 661 8583
E.mail: books@marino.ie

Trade enquiries to CMD Distribution
55A Spruce Avenue
Stillorgan Industrial Park
Blackrock County Dublin
Tel: (01) 294 2556; Fax: (01) 294 2564
E.mail: cmd@columba.ie

© Maeve Flanagan

ISBN 1 86023 090 3
10 9 8 7 6 5 4 3 2 1

A CIP record for this title is available
from the British Library

Cover design by Penhouse Design

Printed in Ireland by
ColourBooks Baldoyle Dublin 13

This book is sold subject to the
condition that it shall not, by way of
trade or otherwise, be lent, resold,
hired out or otherwise circulated
without the publisher's prior consent
in any form of binding or cover other
than that in which it is published and
without a similar condition including
this condition being imposed on the
subsequent purchaser.

No part of this publication may be
reproduced or transmitted in any
form or by any means, electronic or
mechanical, including photocopying,
recording or any information or
retrieval system, without the prior
permission of the publisher in writing.

Extract from 'Memory of my Father'
reproduced by kind permission of the
Trustees of the Estate of Patrick
Kavanagh, c/o Peter Fallon, Literary
Agent, Loughcrew, Oldcastle, Co
Meath, Ireland.

# NELL'S NOVEL

MAEVE FLANAGAN

## ACKNOWLEDGEMENTS

I would like to thank everyone at Marino Books, in particular, Jo O'Donoghue, Rachel Sirr, Eilís O'Donoghue and Seán McMahon.

*For*
*Clíona, Emer and Roisín*

# Chapter One

'Now,' said Heather Connolly. 'What I want for next week is the outline of a novel.' Count me out, thought Nell, who was sitting in the last desk down by the window. 'Aaaannnndd,' Heather continued, 'I also want you to write the first chapter.' She looked around the classroom slowly, making eye contact with all her creative-writing students. 'Try it,' she said. 'You might surprise yourselves.' She smiled and began to pack up her papers and books. The second night of her ten-week creative-writing class was over.

Nell grabbed her folder and jacket and went to the door.

'Are you going over the road, Nell?' Tom called after her.

'Can't this week,' she answered.

'Not even for one?'

'No, I've to be in town in twenty minutes. See you next week.

Nell walked along the corridor to the main door of the building. It was bucketing rain outside. Students from the grind-school end of the complex huddled in the doorway puffing on their Marlboro Lights. She stuffed her manilla folder into her jacket, pulled up the zip and ran to her car.

Nell walked up the stairs into the Westbury lounge. Barbara was there. She had bagged a nice sofa. The pianist was racing through 'Some Enchanted Evening'. Might that do as an opening sentence to Chapter One? she wondered. Stop it, she thought. She crossed the lounge, shook the rain off her jacket and flopped down beside Barbara. Barbara had a small bottle of Glenellen on the table in front of her.

'Here long?' asked Nell.

'No, no, only just got here. Come on, tell us. How did it go? When's the launch? Does Patricia Scanlan have to watch her back?' As she spoke, Barbara raised her finger to the waitress. 'Pint of Guinness,' she said to the hovering adolescent and waved her away again.

'Don't, Barbara,' pleaded Nell. 'I don't know whether I'll go back next week or not.'

'What's wrong, Nell?'

'Barbara,' Nell continued when the waitress was out of earshot. 'For next week she wants, now wait for it, an outline of a novel.' Barbara burst out laughing.

'Pint of Guinness?' said the waitress.

'Here,' said Nell and took a long slug of the Guinness. 'It's easy for you to sit there and laugh, Miss,' said Nell. 'You don't have to do it. You don't even have to try.' Nell started to giggle. 'Barbara, the only thing I have in common with novelists is drinking pints.'

Barbara crooked her finger at the waitress. 'Twenty blue Silk Cut please,' she said.

Nell continued to sip her pint. Barbara was quiet. That was unusual for her. The pianist was gliding through 'I Could Have Danced All Night'. Nell hummed along with him.

'Was it purple or blue Silk Cut you asked for, madam?' asked the waitress. She had a packet of each on her tray.

'Blue,' Barbara snapped at her. She tore off the

8

cellophane, lit a cigarette, and made a perfect smoke ring. 'I have it,' she said, grabbing Nell by the arm. 'I have the perfect idea: set your novel in a school.'

'Don't be stupid, Barbara.'

'Less of the stupid, Nell. Aren't you supposed to write about what you know?'

'Yeah, Barbara, that's *all* I know. That's all we both know. But it's meant to be made up. It's meant to be imaginative.'

'Change the names.'

'People always know, Barbara.'

'Lie. Deny everything.'

God, Barbara had an answer for everything. Nell's Guinness was just landing in her bloodstream. She was getting the giggles. The couch was bouncing.

'Barbara, do you mean put Tom and all them in?'

'Of course. Call him Tim or Terry or something, but yeah, put him in. Change your own name too if you're that scared. Write yourself out of education! Bye bye fixed income. Hello Tuscany. Never mind homework assignments, do it for real.'

It was Nell's turn to call the waitress. 'Same again please,' she said. Then she took Barbara's arm. 'But Barbara, what if I did write it, what if it did get published and you and I and the dogs on the street knew full well that it was only thinly disguised versions of all the creeps we ever met. How could I face people?'

'Ah for God's sake, that's you all over. Cross that bridge when you come to it. What if all that did happen and it was a proper little page-turner and Tom and all his little foibles featured in every single sentence? What would you care? You'd be laughing all the way to the bank.'

'No, she's the Glenellen,' Nell said to the waitress. 'It's

all right, keep the change.' Nell just wanted her to go. 'Right Barbara, supposing I give it a real go; there's no way I'm setting it in a school. Wild horses won't make me write a novel with teachers in it.'

'How are you on porn?'

'What?'

'Could you do a bit of porn? Porn sells.'

'You're not helping one little bit.'

'Nell, grow up. Of course you couldn't write a bit of porn to save your life. Or a blockbuster, or a thriller. If either of us had to write a sexually explicit passage right now we'd probably have to call that little waitress back again to help us. She, at least, had a lovebite on her neck!'

'Point being?' asked Nell.

'Just do it. Do it. Keep going after the night class is over, and for God's sake, send it somewhere and when it comes back, send it somewhere else.'

'Yeah, Barbara, and Mrs Delaney and every Mrs I've ever met will form a vigilante gang and roam Rathmines on winter evenings looking for my blood.'

'Their Starlets would never keep up with your four-wheel drive!'

Barbara blew some more smoke rings. The pianist was charging through 'Everything Free in America, OK By Me in America.

'Course,' said Barbara, 'there's a way round all this. There is the "Barbara Hennessey guide to getting Nell Hynes into print while at the same time sparing her blushes" school of thought.'

'Go on, tell us.'

'Make it all deep and literary. No one will read it. There will be summer schools on you when we're dead. You'll be on the Leaving. There'll be a plaque on your house. But you won't get a penny. So Ms Hynes, which is it to be? Art or money?

Nell and Barbara laughed together. They clinked glasses.

'Money,' said Nell.

'Money,' said Barbara.

They ran down the stairs into Harry Street. It was still raining. Barbara hugged Nell at the top of Grafton Street. 'Keep me posted, Ms Krantz,' she said, grinning.

'My people will talk to your people,' said Nell.

Nell drove home. She put her key in the door and went into the hall. She picked up the fliers from the floor. Critical illness cover and a new Indian takeaway were on offer. She tore them up, binned them and plugged in the iron. She unfolded the ironing board. She ironed the collar and cuffs of the top white shirt in the ironing basket, plugged in the kettle and went up to her boxroom.

There were several piles of copybooks on the desk. There was a ream of A4 paper on the shelf. She pulled out a few pages, selected a pen from her jar and went down to the kitchen. She made a mug of tea and sat at the table. She blew on her tea. She put down her mug, took the top off the pen and wrote, 'My Novel, by Nell Hynes'.

*It was a wild and stormy night. Mists swirled across the vast expanses of the Burren landscape. A carriage drove through the dark Irish countryside. It was bearing the new governess to the castle of Sir Bashel O'Dell. There she would ply her demeaning trade.*

Barbara hasn't a clue, thought Nell. Set my novel in a school? Does she want to get me lynched? Nell stopped writing. She yawned, left the kitchen and went up to bed. So what if I do ditch it all tomorrow, she thought, at least I've made a start. There was a stack of books by Nell's bed, but she wasn't going to read a line. 'When I'm beginning a new novel I find it best not to read at all,' Nell was saying to a woman in the audience as she drifted into sleep. 'I'm always terrified of being derivative.'

# CHAPTER TWO

Why should I blame her that she filled my days
With misery, or that she would of late
Have taught to ignorant men most violent ways . . .

'Miss Hynes?'

'What, Jenny?'

'Are you going to the debs?'

'No.'

'Why not, Miss?'

'Because I'm tired of debs' dances. Now Jenny, tell me, can you remember who is the lady the poet says is making him miserable?'

'Helen of Troy.'

'No, Deborah?'

'Maud, Miss.'

'Maud who, Deborah? Girls, you can't just call her Maud in the Leaving Cert. You have to use both names.'

'Why is she making W. B. Yeats unhappy, girls?'

'He fancies her, but she doesn't fancy him.

'And what's that called?'

'Will you come to our debs, Miss?'

'No.'

'What's that called, Niamh?'

'What?'

'When someone loves someone, and they don't love them back.'

'Not being able to take a hint, Miss.'

'Indeed. But can anyone remember another, fancier name for it? Come on, think. Unreeeee . . . ?'

'Miss, can I go to the toilet?'

'Go on. Can nobody remember?'

' . . . quited love,' said Nell.

'Ah yeah,' said Deirdre.

'Shurrup you. You didn't know that. You're only pretending.'

'I did so.'

'You did not.'

'I did so.'

'How did you know it then, know-all?'

'She told us. Sorry, Miss, Miss Hynes told us yesterday. She said that while Maud did love W. B. very much, she didn't love him in that way. Amn't I right, Miss Hynes?'

'Oh absolutely, Deirdre.'

'Piss off, Deirdre.'

'That's enough.'

'Did he get married, Miss?'

'Yes, but not until he was quite old.'

'But you said he loved Maud all his life, Miss.'

'And so he did.'

'So what did she think, Miss?'

'Who?'

'Mrs Yeats. What did she think of her chap loving Maud on the sly?'

'It wasn't on the sly. It wasn't like that. She was his inspiration. It was all out in the open.'

'Bleedin' slapper. I'd reef her.'

'Did he have kids?'

'Yes. Yeats had a son and a daughter. Come on, we're getting nowhere. Can anybody tell me why the poet

14

compares Maud Gonne to Helen of Troy? What kept you until now?'

'Miss, I felt a bit sick.'

'Will I take her out for some air, Miss?'

'It's last class, Lisa.'

'Nice one, Miss Hynes.'

'Now why all this talk about Helen of Troy?'

'Miss?'

'What, Tracy?'

'If Yeats didn't get married till he was really old . . . '

'Make this quick, Tracy.'

'If he didn't have kids until he was really old, does that mean that Mrs Yeats was much younger than him?'

'She was a good bit younger than him, yes.'

'How much?'

'I don't know exactly. I'll check it. OK? Now why is he talking about Helen?'

'She was a legendary beauty, Miss.'

'She was a what?'

'A legendary beauty, Miss'

'Did I say that?'

'No, Miss, I read it.'

'Where?'

'Here, on this sheet.'

'Where did that sheet come from?'

'I got it from a girl in Honours. She's in the Institute. Do you want it? You can have it if you like. She has loads.'

'No, it's fine. Now for tomorrow . . . '

'Miss Hynes, the bell's gone.'

'For tomorrow,' Nell continued. 'Come on; write it down quickly and then you can go. Select two examples of Yeats's imagery and comment on their effectiveness.'

\*

15

Nell took a trolley instead of a basket. She was going to do a big shop. Can't be running round to Centra when I should be writing Chapter One and the outline, she thought. In the pasta aisle she bought penne, shells, whorls, spaghetti and tagliatelle. She threw in a dozen tins of tomatoes and several tubes of tomato puree. She added tins of salmon, tuna and corn and six two-litre bottles of the shop's own brand of sparkling mineral water. I could write *War and Peace* on that lot, she thought. She skirted the young fellow stacking shelves from a pallet. He had a price gun and he was pricing a girl's chest. 'Ah, Shane, I'll never get them off,' she giggled.

'Course you will.' said Shane. 'I'll get them off for you.' He put down the gun and his fingers advanced under her shop overall.

'Shane,' she squealed.

'Porridge,' said Nell.

'What?' said Shane.

'You're blocking the porridge. I want to get some porridge. Could you pass me out some please?'

'Economy, small, regular or family?'

'Family.'

*

'Dr Liebovitz,' intoned the professor. 'Before I take some questions from the audience, may I just ask you to clarify something which has always intrigued me in your studies of Nell Hynes.'

'Be my guest, Professor.'

'You attach particular significance to the fact that Hynes continued to write to great acclaim into her late eighties, do you not?'

'Why of course, Professor. Longevity in the career of any artist is immensely gratifying for all humankind, but when it's a feature of a major novelist like Nell Hynes who did not publish until she was past forty, it's deeply significant. I feel some of the papers presented here this afternoon have tended to overlook the significance of the smaller things in Hynes's life. In my forthcoming book, *The Shopping Lists of Nell Hynes,* I have attempted to redress that. Consider, for instance, the role of porridge in Nell Hynes's diet. Shopping lists she compiled all the time reveal that she bought enormous quantities of porridge. Porridge, combined with what we could, roughly speaking, call a Mediterranean diet, kept Hynes healthy and creative right up until the very end.'

*

Nell couldn't join the express queue with a full trolley. The woman in front of her had twelve catering pans. At least I'm not letting my standards slip just because I'm being creative, she thought. Can't neglect housekeeping for art. The checkout girl put the 'next customer please' plastic thing down after the twelfth catering pan. She twirled Nell's Jif, rubber gloves, toilet duck, Mr Muscle, Ariel and Lenor around, found the bar codes, and they chugged along to Nell. Nell packed them into carrier bags and filled the trolley.

'£84.98 please.'

'My God,' said Nell.

There were fifteen carrier bags on the path in front of Nell's door. Nell took four into the kitchen. After her last trip she closed the door and picked up that day's flyers.

'I thought I was too young to suffer a stroke,' the bubble

of speech proclaimed from a glamorous woman's mouth. Inside the glossy flyer was a graph. It tabulated the scariest illnesses imaginable along the bottom of the page. At the side of the page were a list of age groups. A red line mounted the graph; it sped along to Nell's age group. Nell tore it up and threw it in the bin. She unpacked the shopping, picked up her jacket and walked down to Luigi's chip shop. 'I'll be Mediterranean tomorrow,' she muttered.

After finishing the last of her smoked cod and chips, she took the tray from her lap and placed it on the floor. She put her feet up on the couch. A nice ruminative stretch wouldn't go amiss before tackling the first chapter; in fact, it might even assist the creative flow.

*

'In previous interviews, Nell, you have frequently praised literary prizes. Cynics might claim that this is no surprise, given the number you have been awarded. But, all personal considerations aside, do you consider the plethora of literary prizes today beneficial to literature?'

'Without a doubt, Melvyn. My views on literary prizes have not changed as a result of winning any. I see the literary prize as a midwife to emerging artists and a valuable sustenance to the existing practitioners of our art.'

Melvyn Bragg was sitting in Nell Hynes's living room. Everything, so far, was going without a hitch.

'Nonetheless, Nell, I'm sure that you would acknowledge that there are many wonderful works which have received none of these plaudits,' said Melvyn. Melvyn was wearing one of his stripey shirts. Nell thought it was the same one he had worn when he had interviewed Beryl Bainbridge.

'I couldn't agree with you more, Melvyn,' said Nell. I would even go so far as to say that many recipients of these prizes have sunk without a trace. It's a fear which haunts me too; who is to say how posterity will deal with me? But, in the final analysis, the impact of prizes for me has been psychological, not monetary.'

'How so?' asked Melvyn.

'Well, Melvyn, when I won the Betty Trask Award, I was just peeping above the parapet, so to speak. Artistical- ly, I was terribly insecure and vulnerable; getting the Betty Trask was a validation; it said to me, "Nell Hynes, you can write, keep going."'

'Is there a difference between prizes, do you think?'

'In my experience, yes, absolutely yes. After my first novel was published and successful, I was terrified I couldn't do it again. Real, nagging doubts set in, Melvyn. I worried that I might just be a flash in the pan, that the second novel was just mediocre. But then along came the Whitbread, just at the right moment; so as far as I'm concerned, prizes have been central to my writing life.'

'They have enabled you to give up teaching too. Has that freedom been central to your writing career?'

'Undoubtedly, Melvyn. Full-time work bleeds all artists dry, none more so than teaching, and while I was no Jean Brodie, I did, nevertheless, try to give of my best. And that took such a toll. Trying to spend several hours every night at the word processor and cope with the demands of full-time teaching became simply impossible.'

Melvyn was smiling at Nell; there was a chemistry between them; she could feel it. Melvyn's big cow's lick was slipping across his forehead; he fingered it carefully back into place. He looked at his clipboard, nodded to the floor manager, then addressed the camera one last time:

'And my thanks to Nell Hynes. Now, that wasn't too much of an ordeal, was it?' he asked Nell. 'No, I shan't stop for coffee. I'll see you tomorrow for the location shots.' Melvyn was on his mobile; within seconds a taxi drew up at Nell's door, he was gone and the men from London Weekend Television were rolling up miles and miles of cable.

*

A ruminative stretch wouldn't have been a bad idea if you had ruminated, but developing that nonsensical Melvyn Bragg daydream is ludicrous. It isn't as if you can spare the time, she thought crossly. The dishes aren't washed, the shopping's not put away and you haven't written a word of Sir Bashel O'Dell. Nell went to the kitchen and scooped up all her tins and jars and bottles. She shoved them into the presses any old way at all. 'To hell with "best before" and "sell by". I can't deal with everything,' she grumbled aloud

She picked up her pen and her A4 page. Now where was I? she thought. OK. The new governess is arriving at a castle in the Burren. So, what'll I call her? Has to be something which sounds authentically old. No Denises or Bernadettes here. Have it: Isabella. Where's she from? Has to be England; the Irish gentry would swoon over an English girl. 'Swoon.' Like the sound of that. Atta girl Nell! You're getting the hang of the language already. What's her background, her social class? Clergymen's daughters usually became governesses. N.N.B. Nell wrote in the margin of her page: do not reread *Jane Eyre*. So what have we? English governess, name Isabella, comes to take up position in Ireland, not a clergyman's daughter.

Isabella knocked timidly on the drawing-room door. 'Come in,' a voice called out from within. Isabella entered the room. Lady Montfieore sat in her chair, an embroidered ottoman at her feet. She worked at her needlepoint. For close stitching Lady Montefiore wore her pince-nez. Isabella stood at the ottoman. Lady Montefiore did not speak; she continued to stitch, though she sensed Isabella's presence. 'You sent for me, Mamma,' she began.

'What I have to say to you will be brief,' Lady Montefiore began. 'You have brought disgrace on this family. Your dalliance with that stable boy has ruined any chance you have of making a suitable alliance with any son of the county's finest families. He of course is dismissed. But, my girl, you'll have to go too. We cannot jeopardise Sophia or Rupert's chances of suitable alliances. With you gone and the lad dismissed we may just have acted in time.'

'But, Mamma, I love him. He loves me. We mean to marry. I shall have my own money when I'm one and twenty. Neither you nor Papa can prevent us.'

'Be quiet this instant. You shall never see a penny of that money. From this day forward you do not exist.'

'But, Mamma, where shall I go?'

'Your father and I have devised a plan. You were quite set on an obscure life of penury with your stable lad. Well, my girl, you shall have exactly that. Your father and I are sending you as governess to the house of our distant cousin Sir Bashel O'Dell. Sir Bashel's castle is in the remotest part of the west of Ireland. There you will work until we send for you. Don't snivel, Isabella. Go now and pack your things.'

Isabella sat at her escritoire. Phelps the footman carried her valises down to the waiting carriage. She tried to compose a short note to her love. Her tears smeared the page and the ink ran. 'My own one,' she wrote, 'I shall never forget you. I *shall find a way for us to be together.' She handed her last florin to Phelps. 'Please see that gets to Barney,' she said, and she stepped into the carriage.*

Nell put down her pen. How would she have got to Ireland in those days? What ports did they use? What type of ship would she have travelled on? Is a novel set in the distant past a good idea? What about research? Sure I know nothing about history. Nell made some tea. Ah sure I'll give it a go, she thought as she sipped.

*'I don't half like lookin' at you, Miss Isabella,' Barney whispered as he unsaddled Isabella's horse. Isabella was not sure if she heard him correctly. 'I don't half like lookin' at you, Miss Isabella,' he said again, this time with more urgency and more confidence. 'You got such lovely eyes.'*

    *'Take that, you dolt,' said Isabella. She was outraged that the fellow had addressed her in such a familiar fashion. As she spoke she cut him with her riding whip. An ugly weal formed on his cheek. Her own violence had shocked her. She studied his face for a moment. Tears filled his eyes. He had beautiful eyes.*

    *'Look, I reacted in haste,' she said, 'but you did deserve it for importuning me so.'*

    *'I know it weren't right for me to address a fine lady so. But I do love you, honest I do. All the time I've been ridin' with you I can't think of nothin' else.'*

    *'Can't you dry your eyes? Or blow your nose or something? Haven't you got a handcherchief?'*

    *'No, Miss Isabella, ain't nothin' here to wipe me nose on 'ceptin' a bit of straw.'*

    *'Well use it then, for pity's sake.'*

    *Her fingers touched the weal. Some force drew her to him.*

*She soothed the hot weal with the tips of her finger. She drew back in horror. She, Isabella Montefiore, was caressing a mere stable lad. Had she lost complete control of herself? His mouth drew nearer to hers. The horses whinnied in their stalls. Isabella started in fright. But she didn't care. She moved to Barney's lips, he moved to her and they kissed a long slow kiss.*

*'I don't half like it when your buzzoms is close, Miss Isabella,' said Barney, growing bolder.*

*Isabella gazed into Barney's blue eyes. Damn! The fellow was coarse. But she had never felt anything like this before. 'Would you like my bosoms even closer, Barney?' she asked. 'Shall I unfasten my stays and let them caress that weal?' Barney smiled. 'Oh yes, Miss Isabella,' he said.*

Nell paused from her writing. She had four pages of A4 covered in longhand. It was nearly midnight. 'Night night, Isabella,' she said, before turning off the lights in the kitchen and climbing the stairs to bed.

# CHAPTER THREE

'We Irish are like the Russians, Melvyn,' said Nell. Immediately she was sorry she had used the phrase: it wasn't hers; she had heard Edna O'Brien saying something of the sort to some English interviewer, years before, on a books programme. She hoped it hadn't been Melvyn. Even if it had been a different interviewer her problems weren't over: Melvyn would want her to expand on it. Edna had sounded really literary when she had said it. Nell felt she just sounded silly. And Edna too had all the attributes to accompany such an elegant phrase. She had a lovely, long, slender neck and a mane of red hair. Nell was dumpy; she had no neck to speak of. Edna had rolled her r's very sexily when she had said 'Irish' and 'Russian'. Nell had to raise her voice above the wind to speak to Melvyn.

'In what way?' asked Melvyn.

'Oh, Melvyn, it's difficult to articulate. One just thinks of Chekhov and all that melancholia and longing, all that yearning to go to Moscow, and one just feels an instant affinity. It's what I call the "samovar-on-the-range syndrome". The two races are just deeply connected; it's a primeval thing.'

Melvyn seemed happy with that. They continued to walk along Sandymount Strand. The crew from London Weekend Television hovered. Nell wore her long Laura Ashley jacket, black denim jeans and stout walking boots.

Dark colours would make her look more writerly, she felt. She had yet to see a novelist on television wearing pastels. 'The sea isn't important in your work, yet you say you walk this beach several times a week. Why is that?'

'Joyce, Melvyn. When I walk along Sandymount Strand I feel the ghosts of Stephen Dedalus, Leopold Bloom and poor little Gertie McDowell. I look across the strand here towards Dun Laoghaire, and beyond that again to Sandycove to the Martello Tower, and I can always picture Buck Mulligan ascending the steps with his shaving bowl in his hand. You see, Melvyn, we Irish writers are haunted by Joyce. He draws us, teases us, dares us to do even greater things with the novel.'

'Are you in any way intimidated by him?'

'Not any longer. I've written him out of my system. At this point in my career he merely empowers me.'

Melvyn and Nell left the beach. They climbed the stone steps to the pathway. At the roadside was a waiting taxi hired by LWT. It whisked them both to a nearby hotel. Over coffee and sandwiches Melvyn explained the rest of the proceedings to Nell.

'Basically, Nell, we have all we need from you. We intersperse the shots in your home with what we've got on the beach. That will make for a more interesting format. We'll do a short biographical sketch to open with. We will also have some pieces from writers who will assess your place in the canon, as it were. We have a short piece already from A. S. Byatt and we're working on some others as well . . . '

*

Nell heard a strange hissing and spitting sound. She was sitting at the kitchen table sipping her coffee while the porridge simmered. She jumped up from the table: the porridge had bubbled up all over the top of the cooker. The bottom of the pot was black. She pulled the pot from the ring. 'Jesus, Mary and Joseph!' she screamed, as the red-hot handle burned deeply into her hand. She grabbed the tea towel, wrapped it round the handle, opened the back door and threw the pot out into the garden. It was raining and the pot sizzled and spat in the centre of the lawn as the big raindrops fell on it. Don't want that thing smelling up the kitchen all day, she thought. She ran her sore hand under the cold tap and set to preparing breakfast for the second time. I never used to daydream, she thought. What's got into me? Surely it should be possible to do a little bit of creative writing without all this nonsense. Melvyn Bragg coming to interview you. I ask you! As if. She was getting really embarrassed as she remembered her little fantasy. That man would only interview people who wrote real books, not someone who has gone to two writing classes and has a few pages of muck sitting on the kitchen table. Even if the Sir Bashel story was finished, and it's a very big if, fancy people like Bragg would curl their lips in disdain at the idea of talking to a writer like you. She flung a handful of Rice Krispies into a bowl, poured more coffee and sat down to breakfast number two.

*

'No, Niamh, I said no and I mean no.'

'But, Miss Hynes, please; it's for me young entrepreneur's project,' Niamh pleaded.

Niamh was standing in the long corridor. She had waylaid Nell on her way to class. She was carrying a big tray of bockety Rice Krispie buns. Nell's hand was still sore and she didn't want to see any more Rice Krispies.

'Niamh, what's an entrepreneur?' asked Nell.

'A businessman, Miss,' said Niamh.

'And what's the most crucial thing for a businessman or woman, Niamh?'

'The marketplace, Miss Hynes.'

'And is accosting teachers on the corridor and expecting them to buy your Rice Krispie buns a real marketplace experience?

'No, Miss, maybe not.' Niamh hadn't a clue what Miss Hynes was going on about, but she felt it was safer to agree.

'The marketplace is harsh, Niamh. It is not full of people ready to buy whatever you take a notion to make, just because they know you.'

'But I have some candles as well, Miss,' she said, putting down her tray to root in a Quinnsworth bag.

'Niamh, I don't want candles or buns. You must accustom youself to the vagaries of the marketplace.'

'The what, Miss?'

'It doesn't matter. Just tell Miss O'Connor that's what Miss Hynes said when she refused to buy your things. Now go to class, you're late.' With a weary sigh, Nell made her way to the classroom.

'Open your books on page seven,' she said, 'and answer question two. If you were listening yesterday you'll be well able to try it. Hurry up, you'll have to read out whatever you have in three minutes.'

'Tracy's hand shot up. 'I'm not answering any questions, Tracy; do it,' said Nell.

'But what if I get it wrong?' Tracy insisted.

'I'll tell you what's wrong when you've written something. You will not have me at your elbow next June; you must try it on your own.'

Tracy selected a pink and a yellow highlighter pen from her huge pencil case. She highlighted the question in pink. She reached into her pencil case again; this time she chose a red biro.

'Anyone got a ruler?' she bellowed.

'Oh, me heart,' complained Rachel.

'You don't need a ruler, Tracy,' said Nell.

Tracy glowered at Nell. She grabbed Ciara's protractor and ruled a gigantic margin.

The classroom darkened suddenly. Nell switched on the lights. Hailstones thundered against the tarmac in the yard. All the heads turned to the window.

'Never mind the hailstones, girls; just get on with the question.'

'Never mind the hailstones, she says,' mimicked Caroline. 'Miss Hynes, you don't have to walk out in them big, mad hailstones. It's OK for you; you've got your car.'

'Two minutes, Caroline, that's all you have left. In two minutes you'll have to start reading the answers.'

Nell sat at a desk at the back of the room. It was easier to keep an eye on everyone from that vantage point. Hailstones bounced against the window pane and the windscreens of the teachers' cars were white.

'Ah, Miss, this is real borin'.'

Nell went to the back of the class again. Tracy was right; it was boring. Nell knew she was boring them rigid herself; she would curl up and die if she were a fly on her own wall. Nell was sure Bryan MacMahon never bored his classes like this; no, it was all delight in learning down in Listowel, a 'Window of Wonder' would open every second in his classes. Did that man never wake up on a dreary November morning and just not want to face another day in a classroom? Apparently not, if the radio programmes were anything to go by. Anyone he ever taught seemed to think he was magic. If any of these girls were asked at some future date for their recollections of Nell Hynes they would surely slate her. And they'd be right, Nell thought. Clumps of hailstones slipped from the bonnets of the teachers' cars and slid on to the tarmac.

Was it because he was creative and talented that MacMahon did a better job? How would Seamus Heaney find Tracy and co? Would he inspire them? He certainly thought beautiful thoughts; they were all near tears when Nell read 'Mid-Term Break' to them for their Junior Cert. But he probably wrote that in a book-lined study far from schoolchildren. How, Nell wondered, were his classroom-management skills? Her own weren't much with this lot; they were sure to be better than Seamus Heaney's. Nell would put money on it: Seamus Heaney would let Niamh, Tracy, Lisa and Rachel out to the toilet at the same time.

'Miss, the bell went.'

'It didn't.'

'It musta went, Miss. Everyone else is out 'cept for us.'

The handle of the classroom door was being pumped up and down; students were jostling outside trying to get into their room. The bell rang.

'See, Deborah?'

'What, Miss?'

'It's only ringing now.'

Fade far away, dissolve, and quite forget
What thou among the leaves hast never known,
The weariness, the fever, and the fret
Here, where men sit and hear each other groan;
Where palsy shakes a few, sad, last gray hairs,
Where youth grows pale and spectre-thin,
                                                    and dies;
Where but to think is to be full of sorrow
And leaden-eyed despairs,
Where beauty cannot keep her lustrous eyes,
Or new Love pine at them beyond tomorrow.


'Miss Hynes,' said Emma, 'that's the third time you've read that stanza aloud and I still don't get it. Emma had her pencil poised. She wanted to take copious notes on what the poem meant.

'Emma,' said Nell. 'Do you think you understand Shelley?'

'Yes, Miss Hynes.'

'Did you understand him when we were reading him for the first time?'

'No, Miss Hynes.'

'Well it's the same with Keats. Have some patience, give yourself a chance; it's only day two.'

Nell nodded at Jackie. 'Any ideas?' she asked her.

'Haven't a clue, Miss,' she answered. Nell did a quick sweep of the fifth-year class with her eye. Nobody looked ready to venture an opinion as to what Keats was saying in stanza three of 'Ode to a Nightingale', that was, except Kate and her gang. There would be plenty of time for them; better to check with the more reticent students first. Kate and her gang were just a blur; their seats did not come within the range of Nell's spectacles. But Nell could

30

sense them filling up with air; pre-speech sounds were already coming from their quarter. Kate's gang consisted of Kate herself, Sorcha, Sinéad and Cliona.

Nell usually started with a novel in fifth year; this year the prescribed novel was *Hard Times*. But this September Nell didn't have the stomach for *Hard Times*. *Hard Times* deserved to be left to January's gloom. Outside the classroom windows an Indian summer was in full swing. The groundsman was whizzing around on the big mower, and wasps gorged on leftovers in the students' discarded yogurt cartons on the classroom-window ledges. She began instead with Shelley.

'Close your books and listen,' she said. 'I want to tell you a little about this man before we begin to read his poems. The man I am going to tell you about is much more interesting than Kurt Cobain, River Phoenix, John Lennon or Bob Marley, and in his own time he had much more influence than any of those men. His name was Percy Shelley.'

Nell settled her bottom on the radiator and looked around the room. Emma was writing furiously. Let her, thought Nell. 'Girls, Shelley was a rebel, and I don't mean the kind who doesn't wear the correct shoes to school,' she continued, eyeing Cliona's Doc Martens. 'Shelley shocked the society of his time. He was expelled from Oxford because he wrote a pamphlet called *The Necessity of Atheism*.'

Kate had begun to sit up straight. Sorcha in the desk behind her was showing signs of coming to life too.

'Shelley eloped with a sixteen-year-old girl. He lived in communes in England and Europe.' Nell continued to fill the class in on what she knew of Shelley's life. At the back of the room Sorcha's eyes were dilating. 'Cool,' she exhaled, as Nell told the class of Shelley's liaison with Mary Shelley, who had written Frankenstein. Sorcha was a touch Transylvanian herself. She wore pale make-up, had eight studs in both ears, didn't wear a school tie and under her white blouse peeped a black T-shirt.

> 'I could lie down like a tired child
> And weep away this life of care
> which I have borne and still must bear'

Nell would have continued a little longer had it not been for Kate. Kate went into orbit. 'Miss, that is so incredible,' she squealed.

'Why?' asked Nell.

'It's just, just, just so emotional.'

'Go on,' said Nell.

'I don't know. It's kinda hard to explain . . . it's just, like . . .'

'He has had enough, Miss; he can't take any more, Miss,' piped up Cliona.

'Go on, keep going,' said Nell.

'He just wants to scream and sob and shriek and pound his fists, Miss,' said Cliona.

'And does he tell us why?' asked Nell.

'No, Miss.'

'Do we need to know?' asked Nell.

'Not really. We can all can understand, everyone feels like that sometimes,' answered Sorcha.

'Miss Hynes, did he kill himself?' asked Kate. She drew her thin neck out to its full length. It was deathly pale and almost completely covered in black leather thongs.

'What's making you think of suicide, Kate?'

'The line, "This life of care that I have borne and still must bear",' she replied.

'No, he didn't kill himself. He is in despair here but he didn't kill himself. Now for the less interesting part: tonight I want you to read the whole poem. It isn't all as easily understood as "I could lie down like a tired child", and I want you to underline in pencil anything you don't understand.'

Emma was in good form the second day Nell was doing Shelley. She had read the poem; she had lots of material underlined. She wrote busily as Nell explained to the class. When she had finished filling in the glossaries in her poetry book, she checked all that Nell had told the class in the little exam guide she always kept by her poetry book and her A4 pad. Emma's mother wanted her to do medicine; she needed millions of points. Cliona, Sorcha, Sinéad and Kate were sulking; they were cross with Nell. They had read the poem at home, but nothing had hit them quite like the lines they had looked at yesterday. Miss Hynes had taken the best bit to lure the class into Shelley; they felt duped. They fiddled with their earrings and doodled on their folders.

'Jackie,' said Nell, '"I am one whom men love not". What does that suggest to you?'

'Nobody likes him, Miss.'

'Yeeesss. Anyone like to add to that?'

'He's not popular, Miss,' said Debbie.

'True, and does that bother him, do you think?'

'Maybe, a bit maybe,' said Debbie.

Kate was breathing heavily. She looked over at Debbie in disbelief. 'The man couldn't give two figs about being popular,' she hissed.

'Something to say, Kate?' asked Nell. She stole a glance at Debbie first. Debbie seemed not to have noticed Kate's contempt.

'He doesn't want to fit in to society or be a lick, but he still feels the pain of isolation,' Kate said. 'The world's beautiful, but that doesn't make him feel better,' she continued.

The next morning, Nell decided it was time to introduce the class to Keats. She was hoping that the Indian summer would last while they were reading Keats; she would have liked some sun as the ideal backdrop, at least while they were studying the odes. But instead they got rain, wind and hailstones. The poor little nightingale would sing for the first time in her fifth-year class on a day when the sky was grey and hailstones were swirling around the schoolyard like plastic beads.

'"My heart aches",' she began. Sinéad was alert at the very mention of an aching heart. Sorcha's eyes grew wide when she heard the word 'opiate'. Emma was happy as a sandboy because she had lots of explanations to fill in. She scribbled in the margins of her poetry book; she expanded on her points in her A4 pad and finally she verified all she had noted in her little guide.

'Why does he want to "fade far away".That just doesn't make sense to me,' Emma insisted.

'I am not telling you. There are no complicated allusions here; think for yourself. Why does anybody ever want to run off?' Nell looked around the class. There were several hands up. 'Avril?'

'He wants the nightingale to take him away because he's unhappy,' she ventured.

'Yes, well done. Now can anybody tell me why someone might want to leave the world?'

A mournful chorus wailed from Sorcha's row: 'It's all so awful,' they said.

'What's "all so awful"?'

'Life, Miss Hynes, life,' said Sorcha.

'Everything's rotting, all the beauty and everything,' Sinéad added.

'Even thinking is too painful,' Cliona expanded.

'Is that the answer, Miss Hynes?' asked Emma.

'I am afraid it is, Emma,' said Nell.

'Does he want to get really drunk and escape all the pain in the world?' asked Kate.

'Yes, Kate, he does, but he rejects that as a solution. He comes up with a different and better way of escaping. Who can see it?' There was no answer. 'Ah, come on,' said Nell, 'it's easy. Who did I say was the god of wine?'

'Bacchus,' said Emma.

Then the bell rang. 'Now, tonight read that stanza again. Pick the exact references to drink as an escape, then locate his rejection. After that, try to see what he comes up with as a better means of leaving the world.'

# Chapter Four

Nell came in the door from school. She dropped her school bag on the floor and made a big mug of coffee. She sat at the kitchen table and thought about her assignment for the writing class. The A4 pages with the beginnings of the governess story were still on the table. But they were trash; there was no way she would bring them to the writing class. I'll just kill off Isabella and Sir Bashel, she thought. She tore the pages up into tiny pieces and burned them in an old ashtray. My God, she thought, giggling in the quiet kitchen, look at the power I have! I give life and I take it away again! Though that's not strictly true in the case of Sir Bashel: he hadn't really featured yet in my tale.

While she ate her dinner, she contemplated the dilemma precipitated by her characters' demise: If she killed off Sir Bashel and Isabella, what would she have to bring to the writing class? And what could she write that might be developed into something serious long after the ten-week writing class was over?

She had some fresh A4 pages by her plate, and in between forkfuls of smoked fish and stir-fry vegetables she conducted a small brainstorming session. A school scenario was still definitely out of the question. She wrote the word 'school' on her page – largely to take the bare look from it – then she crossed it out. She jotted down some possible names for characters. Whatever Nell's characters might do, or say, she wanted them to have names she was comfortable with. She wanted their names to sound real to her, yet not too close to names of people she knew. 'N.B. Look in phonebook,' she wrote into a big bubble. 'Lara? Kara? Dane?or Russell?' she continued into a second bubble. Almost immediately, she scribbled a dirty great 'X' across that bubble. Those names were too Sky mini-series-ish. She would stick to Jack, Brendan and Dermot and whatever the women's equivalents might be. Potential names for characters formed two small columns on her page; she highlighted these columns in red and pink, using the pens she had confiscated from Tracy at school. That much accomplished, Nell made tea.

Stage two was more daunting: what genre should she use? 'Genre?' she wrote with her fountain pen. She drank her tea and considered it all ruefully. The next writing class would be on Monday and, as yet, Nell had nothing written, not even a sketchy draft which might, if dickied up, be passed off as 'work in progress'. That was the writer's term for it, wasn't it? She smiled as she remembered it. Her own work in progress was just a small heap of charred paper in an ashtray. If the worst came to the worst she could bring Sir Bashel and Isabella back to a temporary life for the next writing class; then, at least, she wouldn't turn up empty-handed. Whatever comments the story might get could prove useful too in the larger scheme of things. And it was the larger scheme of things which really concerned her.

Barbara had been spot on when she spoke of the necessity of Nell continuing to write after the ten-week class was over. That was exactly what Nell wanted to do. She wanted to create something – nothing fancy, just a story for grown-ups, with a beginning, a middle and an end. She wanted to produce something which men and women would go into a bookshop and finger for a few moments, read a few lines of, part with five or six pounds for, take home and read and not feel they had been cheated. She had done that thousands of times herself since she was a teenager. But consuming the printed word was such a simple act; trying to be in on even the most downmarket part of the creation process seemed almost impossible.

Nell filled the sink and washed the dinner dishes and saucepans; a scullion, that's what she was, better suited to pot-walloping than writing novels. She took off her rubber gloves and draped them over the gleaming cups, glasses and cutlery. Leaving the kitchen without her A4 page, she went into the living room to watch some soaps. But the phone rang. Nell guessed it might be Barbara. It was unusual for Barbara to let several days go by without calling, but she had probably been excercising some extra restraint to enable Nell to create. It was Barbara and she wanted an update.

'Nell,' she said breezily, 'surprised you're answering. Thought I might just leave a "Hello" on the answering machine. Now, I won't delay you, but just tell me, how's the novel?'

'Barbara, don't use that word.'

'What word?'

'Novel, Barbara, novel.'

'Why?'

'A novel, Barbara, is something like *War and Peace* or *Ulysses.*'

Barbara gave one of her big laughs. 'Oh, so that's how it is, is it?'

'And what's that supposed to mean?'

'Ah don't be so precious and tempermental. I only rang

to say, "Hello, how's it going? Have you written even a couple of paragraphs of the great exposé of the Irish secondary school?" And if you have, I wanted to wish you luck. I didn't ask for a talk on what constitutes a novel. Andy O'Mahony does that better than you any day and I can get the ironing done at the same time.'

Nell relaxed a little; it wasn't fair to be crabby with Barbara. 'Sorry, Barbara, I didn't mean to bite the nose off you. I am trying to write. I had a few pages done but I ditched them, they were awful. And before you ask, there wasn't a teacher, nun, brother or schoolchild in it.'

'And why not? Why won't you listen to your Auntie Barbara?'

'You know why. I told you in the Westbury.'

'Yeah, and I told you then and there you were barking up the wrong tree. Nell, don't be such a coward! Use a pseudonym, have a co-educational school with a male principal. There are ways round all the problems you insist on seeing. If you had taken my advice on Monday you'd be on a roll now – pages done, no time to answer the phone, and there wouldn't be a sign of writer's block!'

'I'd have to be a writer to experience writer's block.'

'God! We're having a lovely writerly wallow, aren't we?'

'Ah, Barbara, stop, please. You can't tease me round to your way of thinking.'

'No, but I can try. Anyway, tell me, pet. What was the story you ditched like?'

Nell took a deep breath, swallowed a few times . . .

'Nell, are you still there?'

'Yes, I'm still here. I'm just trying to think how I might describe it. It was about a young, aristocratic English-woman who fell in love with a stable lad. The result of this liaison was that she was disowned by her family. As punishment for her transgressions she was sent to the west of Ireland, to the castle of a distant cousin, where she was expected to work as a governess.'

'But Nell, you don't read books like that; how would you know how to write one?'

Nell felt utterly deflated. Barbara was right. Nell played with the cord of the telephone as she thought. Can't write about what I know because I'm too scared. I haven't got what it takes to write really good, well-crafted popular fiction, and I haven't the talent to deliver the heavy-duty, thought-provoking, life-changing stuff. A gardening group met across the corridor from Heather Connolly's creative-writing class. Nell had seen them dragging boughs from the boots of their cars. That was the group she ought to have joined.

'Have I hurt your feelings, Nell? You've gone very quiet.'

'No, no, you've just set me thinking, that's all.'

'Nell, you're not to think of giving up. You can do it. But do you know what I think is holding you back?'

'What?' Nell asked flatly.

'Newspapers. All those quality Sundays that you read with all the book reviews. The worse thing you could do to yourself is keep reading those things.'

'I'll bear it in mind, Barbara.'

'Ah, come on, Nell. I'm serious. You admire all those old Hermiones and Pierses and whatever they say about this novel or that biography. If you can't deliver in two days flat the sort of stuff you think they'd admire, you try for something you know nothing about, then you get all down in the dumps when it doesn't work out. They're only a crowd of show-offs. Do what you're good at. Write about what's under your nose.'

'We'll have to agree to differ about that.'

'Are you finished writing for this evening?'

'I didn't even get started. I'm not going to now. I'm going to sit down and watch lots of soaps. I haven't seen any for ages. I'm going to loll on the couch and forget all about writing.'

'Good for you. Coffee on Saturday, maybe?'

'Love to, but I'm meeting Miriam. I haven't seen her for months.'

'Right so, Nell, but give me a ring now, won't you?'

'Course I will.'

Nell took the phone off the hook, plugged in the television and draped herself along the couch. She settled the cushions and balanced the remote control on her tummy; the advertisements were still on; she hadn't missed any of *Coronation Street*. There had been a time when she would never have dreamed of missing an episode of *Coronation Street*, *Brookside* or *Eastenders*. When she was a keen soap fan Nell always took the phone off the hook while they were on; not everyone who knew her remembered not to disturb her when she was watching her favourite programmes. But one day, like someone who has binged once too often on a favourite food and swears never to eat another bite of it again, Nell decided to stop watching soaps. It wasn't a snooty, high-moral-ground decision; she just felt that she couldn't bear to see another one.

Some people Nell knew who claimed never to watch television had five or six complicated sweaters knitted each winter, or they were reading their way through libraries. Nell had nothing to show for her newfound leisure time, but that didn't bother her; she was merely embracing a different kind of sloth.

'*Coronation Street*, sponsored by Cadbury's, the nation's favourite,' said a voice. That was new to Nell. But then came the old signature tune she loved – the northern brass band playing: 'Da dada, dadadaaa'. Nell hummed along with the tune. It didn't matter at all that Nell had missed so many episodes of *Coronation Street*: she worked with lots of fans of the programme so she still knew what had been happening.

Nell had planned to make a quick dash to the bathroom during the commercial break but she changed her mind when she saw what came up on the screen. Instead of a still of the cobbled streets of Weatherfield there was a chocolate street. Two chocolate women in Hilda Ogden pinnies and curls gossiped at a chocolate street corner. A chocolate cat did its chocolate best to be feline and curl languidly on chocolate roof slates. The brown colour everywhere made Nell's stomach heave; it spooked her slightly too. Had they all gone mad at Granada? she wondered. She was relieved when the credits rolled in the usual way, the music played and the fluffy and real marmalade cat lolled in the sun. But then the word 'Cadbury' filled the screen against a brown chocolate background, milk was added to the chocolate and the two colours swirled together into a revolting mess; Nell really wanted to get sick at the sight.

She zapped the remote control; she wanted to see if anyone at the BBC had been tinkering with the visuals at Eastenders; but everything was fine there: the Thames was looping and curving through India dock, Surrey dock; on and on it went down to Bermondsey and Greenwich. The bridges, too, were where they ought to be. Behind the bar at the Queen Vic, Grant Mitchell was swelling out of a black T-shirt; there was spittle at both sides of his mouth: 'Get it sor'id,' he bellowed at Tiff. Nell rearranged her cushions and watched Eastenders, glad that some things, at least, remained the same.

At half-past eight, she reached into her school bag. She might as well correct the excercises she had brought home if she was not going to tackle a new novel; the 'half in love with easeful death' brigade would be clamouring to know how she rated their questions on Shelley. She pulled out the wad of multicoloured pages. They were excellently answered; it was they who should be contemplating writing careers, not Nell, she reflected. She made some minor adjustments to Cliona's exuberance, toned down Kate's purple prose, and in the margin of Sorcha's she wrote, 'Avoid analogies with your own life. This would be more appropriate in the essay on Paper One, provided, of course, there is an essay on abuse, persecution and suffering.' Sorcha had analysed the imagery in Shelley's poetry very well, but when it came to discussing the 'emotional intensity', she had written two paragraphs railing at her mother.

Nell didn't have a big wad of excercises from the sixth years. Most of them didn't do homework; they were working in supermarkets and didn't have the time, or were too tired. She flew through their excercises, correcting some of the spellings. If she corrected every one there would be more red biro than students' writing. She went into the kitchen and made a cup of tea. Her A4 brainstorming page was still on the table but she turned her back to it. The kettle bipped on the counter top; Nell scalded the teapot, threw in a teabag and half-filled the pot.

Waiting for the tea to draw she thought again of the changed *Coronation Street* and how dreadful it would be to live in a brown world peopled by strange, small brown people. She poured herself a cup of tea and began to sip, but her thoughts insisted on returning to the chocolate world. 'I might just jot down a few of these feelings on my page,' she said aloud in the quiet kitchen. She poured a second cup and sat down at the table. But it was not single buzzwords which came to her this time: whole sentences flowed from her pen. Maybe, at last, this was it!

*It was an ordinary day just like any other. I left my two-bedroomed duplex apartment in Rathmines at 7.30. It was a sunny June morning and as I walked into Rathmines Road I felt good. I hailed a bus and ten minutes later I got off at the top of Grafton Street. That was my usual weekday routine. Leave the apartment early, avoid the traffic and take breakfast in town before heading for my office. I walked into Grafton Street, bought an* Irish Times *from my usual man outside Bewley's and went inside for some breakfast. I liked Bewley's before eight in the morning – it hadn't yet begun to get noisy or hot. It was also too early for the usual quota of weirdos: the woman who invited other customers to prayer meetings hadn't appeared. Neither had the man who spent his time stirring endless sachets of sugar into one small cup of tea and talking to himself frantically as he stirred. I didn't have the place to myself, but the other customers wouldn't bother me; they were like me – workers, anxious for a quiet breakfast and a quick glance through the paper before another busy day. I sat into a nice upholstered corner seat, sipped my coffee, slit my sticky bun in two, buttered it and looked at the paper.*

Nell stopped writing. What she had so far wasn't riveting but she had made a start. The creative juices were beginning to flow. And she hadn't got bogged down in all that narrative-technique, authorial-voice nonsense. The straightforward first-person narrator was simplicity itself: it would do splendidly to unfold a profound tale just as effectively as a simple one; the secret was in the writing!

*Suddenly I felt strange knots of tension form in my stomach. Tiny capsules of acid seemed to explode in my entrails. I felt giddy and dizzy. I wanted to leave the restaurant, leave this horrible sensation behind. But what if it came with me, following me to work, keeping me company for the rest of the day? Bewley's stained-glass windows spun above me; the whole room swam before my eyes and I felt I couldn't breathe. I had a horrible sense of foreboding. Turbocharged butterflies fluttered through my stomach. I tried to focus again on the paper but the lines of print jumbled together and I couldn't decipher them. Voices rang in my ears. What if all this showed on my face? Would the other customers notice and wonder who the strange woman was who looked so terrified? Might I now be seen as another of those weirdos who behaved strangely in public places? How would I get to work, and when and if I made to the office, could I keep the strange sensations under wraps sufficiently to do a day's work? Would I make a show of myself at the office? And then the real nightmare started: Bewley's interior drained completely of colour, the deep-wine wallpaper with the small, oriental women turned to brown in an instant; the cream-and-green floor tiles turned to brown too. I looked around the restaurant: all the other customers were turning brown and shrinking to dwarfish sizes. I had to get out of there, and sharp. I stood up from the table. A waitress was approaching me. She was a full-size young woman, wearing the normal waitress's black dress and white apron. She looked foreign. She walked towards me. I was reassured to see how*

45

*ordinary she was. 'Senora,' she said, 'you are OK?'*

*'I'm fine,' I replied. 'It's just the heat.' I smiled at her. She put her tray on my table and started to clear away my things. She wiped the table with a blue J-cloth, but through her pink fingers I could see the edges of the cloth turing to brown, the brown travelled through her fingers, into her hand, up her wrist, and her uniform changed colour too. I looked at her in terror. Brown flowed from her nostrils, eyesockets; every orifice oozed brown. Soon, she too was completely brown. I ran from the restaurant; I had never felt so frightened in all my life.*

Nell had run out of pages. She went to her boxroom and pulled a few from her ream. She hurried downstairs again, anxious not to lose a moment's creativity. She could feel it in her bones. Yes! This was the one. This would really create a stir. It probably wouldn't sell at all, but it would certainly get the heavy-duty treatment! She sat on the last step of the stairs hugging her A4 pages to her chest. She could picture it all; her book would take the literary establishment by storm!

*

'The Irish really are the flavour of the moment, aren't they? What with this latest novel I can't help wondering if there's any stopping them.'

'*Brown World* is a tour de force, quite simply a tour de force,' said a deep, female voice in low, fruity tones. 'Instead of subjecting us to adolescent posturings disguised as fiction, Hynes has lived for forty years and then written. She has a rich seam to mine, and the talent to do it.'

'She is somewhat unusual for an Irish writer in terms of style, isn't she?' queried a male voice.

'Yes, absolutely,' responded a third critic. 'There's a complete dearth of wordiness, of lyricism, of that poetic prose that the Irish so excel at. The style is bare, spare, almost laconic; details are kept to an absolute minimum. I mean, for instance, we don't even know the main character's name.'

'Quite, it puts one in mind of Kafka and K.'

'Yes, indeed, Kafkaesque,' chorused several critics.

'In fact, it's Kafkaesque in more ways than one. The whole collapse of the main character's world is very reminiscent of *The Trial*.'

'I don't see it quite that way myself. In *Brown World* I see Hynes as the chronicler of the *Zeitgeist*; the woman's world becomes an alien place; she is lost and alone; she doesn't live in a police state like some of the former communist countries. The fact that this happens in a democracy makes her tale much more powerful.'

'Her disintegration is personal rather than societal?'

'Absolutely. It's an astonishingly powerful metaphor for the alienation that is life in the dying days of the twentieth century.'

'Germaine, would you attach any significance to the main character's being female?'

'None whatsoever,' said an Australian accent. 'This Hynes woman hasn't a feminist bone in her body. *Brown World* absolutely does not address patriarchy in any way. It's probably the most phallocentric novel I've read in quite some time. Having said that, maybe that's no bad thing because it is, to use your phrase, a tour de force, a linguistic and thematic tour de force.'

'Come, come, Germaine,' said the woman with the fruity voice, 'surely you see some significance in the writer's being a woman?'

'I refuse to discuss that hoary old chestnut. It's a wonderful book, I am sick to death of being invited on arts programmes and being expected to extoll some twaddle because it's written by a feminist, or condemn something powerful because the woman who wrote it had no feminist street cred that we know of. I don't know who this Hynes woman is. I don't give a monkey's if she struggles into a whalebone corset every morning. She has written a bloody good book . . . '

'I am going to have to stop you there, Germaine,' said a voice. It was Mark Lawson!

*

'Get up off that stairs, Nell Hynes, and get into that kitchen and keep writing, 'cos if you don't, neither Mark Lawson nor Germaine Greer will ever discuss your work. Keep your imagination for your oeuvre!' said the sensible voice in Nell's head.

'Yes,' replied Nell to her sensible voice and went back to the kitchen. She stretched herself; she had been sitting for a long time and she was getting stiff. But she was very pleased. Although despondency had clouded the early part of the evening, productivity had been the hallmark of its later hours. It was after midnight; she had school next day, but the dishes were washed, homework was all corrected, and she had seen *Coronation Street*. Best of all was the little stack of A4 pages on the table, each one filled with her close, neat handwriting. And there would be even more, she thought, if I stopped daydreaming. She was resolved; the new novel would be called *Brown World*. She would not bring it to the writing class but would work away quietly at it herself at home, and when she had a couple of thousand words she would submit it to publishers herself. She would scribble out the Sir Bashel and Isabella story again, add another little bit, and that was what she would bring to Heather Connolly's class.

It was well past her usual time for bed and she was exhausted, but there was one little thing she needed to do to be prepared for school the next day. She went into the sitting room and rooted through the bookshelves. Selecting two volumes of poetry, she placed them on top of her school bag; there was no way she would forget them in the morning. I think the fifth years could do with a little Dickinson and Plath, she thought. Emma would be furious: neither poet was on their course, but what the heck? Would she, Nell Hynes, author, with two novels on the go, let that deter her?

*

Break-time was a joke. It wasn't a real break from work at all. Nell left her classes and went to the staffroom. It was almost impossible to get in the door; a dozen or so girls were waiting outside. Tracy and Niamh were there, clutching their stomachs and groaning. 'We're so sick, Miss Hynes,' they said. 'We probably won't be at English this afternoon.'

'I'd be sick too if I came out without any breakfast and then sat for forty minutes in a smelly toilet, smoking.'

Tracy and Niamh put on their most hurt expressions. 'You're so mean, Miss Hynes,' they wailed, 'but will you send Mrs Kinsella out to us. We need to ask her permission to go home.'

'No, I'm not disturbing her break. You'll both survive until half-past ten.'

The junior hockey team was lining up outside the door too. One tiny player was already wearing her goalie's shin pads and taking wild swings with her hockey stick in the narrow passage. Nell placed her bag high on her chest like a riot shield, pressed past the girls, opened the staffroom door and went inside. The photocopier was whirring, and it wouldn't stop either to judge by the queue forming beside it.

'Nell,' called Olivia Colleran. She had two mugs of coffee in front of her, and she patted the cushion of the empty seat beside her.

'You're an angel,' said Nell. 'I couldn't have faced that queue at the boiler.'

Nell sat down beside Olivia. 'Well, how's the writing class going?' she asked.

'Don't mention writing, Olivia. I'm at my wits' end with it.'

A4 pages fluttered into their laps. They looked up. The pages had come from Betty O'Connor. 'Thanks, Betty,' they called after her, but she was gone, already at the other end of the room, dropping pages into the laps of all her colleagues as she went.

'Merciful God, does she ever stop?' asked Olivia. 'What has she given us today, I wonder?'

'I don't know and I don't care. I want to drink my coffee and chat in peace,' said Nell. She folded the page in half. She would slip it into the bin on her way to class.

The photocopier was still whirring. A young man in the corner was showing a video on investing a retirement lump sum. The sound was low; he sat all alone with his clipboard.

'Rich Tea, Nell?' asked Olivia.

'No, I think I'll chance the Marietta.'

'So tell us, Nell. You're not getting off that lightly. What's happening at the writing class? Poems? Plays? Novels?'

'Well, I suppose what she is trying to do is cater for every taste. She will do poems and plays, but at the moment she has us writing the outline and Chapter One of a novel.'

'A whistle-stop tour of all the genres,' laughed Olivia. 'But tell me, Nell, is your story set in our school? Is there a woman in it called Betty who does a leaflet drop every day when we're trying to drink our coffee?'

'It will have nothing to do with schools at all. I don't want to end up in the High Court.'

'Well that's a terrible shame. Think of what Lucy and Betty, called something else of course, would add to a novel; it would be positively Gothic.' Olivia prodded Nell's shin with her shoe. 'Wouldn't it?' she insisted.

'Yeah, that's what scares me.' Then she laughed. 'The Irish are such a litigious race,' she said in a posh, writerly voice. 'It's easy for you to suggest all kinds of daring to me, Olivia. Unlike you, I don't have the cushion of a second income.'

'True,' acknowledged Olivia.

'I navigate the bark of life singly,' said Nell, really getting the giggles this time.

Olivia laughed too. 'Did you just make that up now?' she asked.

'No,' said Nell, 'it's from a film, and not even a good one.'

'What film? I can't say I recognise it myself.'

'*Three Men and a Little Lady*.'

'I saw it but I don't remember that.'

'Do you remember the dowdy schoolmarm. Fiona Shaw

played her. Well, she had her eye on Tom Selleck, and to let him know the path to her affections was clear, so to speak – God I'm beginning to sound like her myself – that's what she said to him: "I navigate the bark of life singly."'

'Is this a private conversation, or can anybody join?' asked Patsy Waldron.

'It's not in the least private,' said Olivia. 'Sit down there. I'm just trying to give Nell a bit of advice on her writing career, but she won't take it. I think she should write a novel and set it in this school. This school is stranger than fiction anyway; it's asking to be written about.'

'But sure she couldn't do that,' said Patsy. Patsy never rocked any boats. 'There would be all sorts of legal implications.'

'Now,' said Nell, sticking her tongue out at Olivia, 'listen to Patsy. Or better still, go over to Ted Falvey and ask him why isn't he painting a series of canvases based on life in our school.'

'I don't see why you should pick on just one branch of the arts to bring the quirks of school life to the public. Let the visual arts make their contribution, I say.'

Olivia was in great form now, laughing her head off. Patsy Waldron was getting very uneasy. Patsy had no sense of humour and she never really knew how to take Olivia. She left Nell and Olivia and stuck her head into her locker.

'Picture it, Nell, a full gallery of Ted Falvey's canvases: axemen running amok, gallows and guillotines, children slaying adults and adults slaying children. All the faces would be faces from our school, with blood, guts and gore everywhere!'

'Come on, it's nearly time.'

Olivia and Nell got up. Olivia crossed the room to the young sales rep who was still sitting alone. 'Young man,' she said to him, 'do you see any man or woman in this room who looks sixty-five?'

'No,' he replied nervously.

'No you don't,' said Olivia, 'because there isn't one, not one single one. Furthermore, there isn't even anybody near to early retirement. I myself have a few miles on the clock, but I still have a long way to go before I can wonder how best to invest my lump sum, so why don't you go away and come back in fifteen years.'

'Olivia,' said Nell, tugging at her sleeve, 'he's only doing his job.'

'Nell, don't worry about his feelings. He'll be off selling windows next week. You and I and all the others will still be here. Showtime next class?'

'I haven't forgotten. Just let's get them settled first.'

'Sure, just knock on the partition when you're ready.'

# CHAPTER FIVE

'Good,' said Nell, when she opened the door of the first-year class; they had stacked the desks along the sides of the large room as Nell had instructed them. Some desks remained in the centre, but those desks would be needed. Nell called the roll and went to do a quick costume and prop check. The class were putting on a scene from *Henry IV, Part One*. They were far from word-perfect and as a spur to their efforts they were going to show what they had done to the first-year class next door. Nell walked quickly through the room. There was a buzz of talk as the actors repeated their lines.

'Now,' said Nell, 'the important thing is not to giggle. We're not doing in the hall if there's giggling. Remember, too, not to be thrown when Mrs Colleran's class laughs, and they will laugh if you do it properly. Now, serving wenches, come here please.' In Shakespeare's text there was only one hostess in the inn at Eastcheap, but in the inn in Nell's class there were three. She wanted to use as many of the thirty pupils as possible. Lisa, Audrey and Martina had found long dresses, and they were wearing aprons and shower caps.

'That's grand,' said Nell. 'But Audrey, I'm a little worried about your dress. It's very fancy for a serving wench.'

'It's my sister's old debs dress; it's the only long dress I could find.'

'Leave it for the moment. Now pull those desks into groups of three; and yokels, where are the yokels? Yokels, sit at the tables.'

Fifteen girls sat at their tables, and the serving wenches practised serving them. 'Mine's a pint of Bud, and the lady'll have a pina colada.'

'Stop that. That's exactly the sort of messing I don't want,' said Nell. 'Now remember, all you have to do is "oooh" and "aaah" at Sir John Falstaff's lies.'

'Can we clink our glasses, Miss Hynes?'

'Who still has a glass?' Two hands went up. 'After all I said about no glasses.'

'Sorry, Miss Hynes.'

'Nathalie and Rebecca, go up quick to the Home Economics room and beg Mrs Hughes for a big sheet of tinfoil.'

'It's OK, Miss Hynes,' shouted Lisa. Lisa was struggling to put a big cushion into the waistband of her leggings. She had cotton wool covering her hair. Lisa was Sir John Falstaff. 'I've tinfoil here,' and she whipped out a large dish. 'I made a lasagne in Home Economics.' She ripped the tinfoil from the plate.

'Now, cover those glasses quickly,' said Nell. 'Make them into pewter tankards immediately.'

'Can we light the candles, Miss Hynes?' There were candles stuck into old wine bottles on every table.

'If you're good for Mrs Colleran's class today, and if you're good enough to do it in the hall, then and only then will we light the candles. For the moment just pretend they are lighting. Lisa and Jackie, are you two ready?'

'Yes, Miss,' they answered.

'Now, all of you just remember that Mrs Colleran's

class doesn't know the play. Speak slowly. Falstaff, you're a liar. Prince Henry knows you're telling lies, and so do the yokels in the inn. Wait for the lies to sink in with the other class. Do not continue speaking until they have stopped laughing. Right, girls at the back, knock on the partition, and Jane, music please.'

Jane released the pause button on the tape recorder; the partition doors opened; Olivia Colleran's class swivelled round and faced Nell's group; there were a few small giggles but the music drowned them out. Sir John Falstaff entered and came to the centre of the stage, Lisa kept her hands on her cushion paunch, and Jackie addressed her:

'Here comes lean Jack. Here comes bare bone.'

'Laugh,' Nell mouthed at the yokels. They laughed. Olivia's class picked up their cue and laughed too.

'How now my sweet creature of bombast. How long is't ago since thou sawest thine own knee?'

'My own knee?' squeaked Lisa in a decent attempt at pique. 'When I was about thy years, Hal, I was not an eagle's talon in the waist – I could have crept into any alderman's thumb-ring.' She took one hand from her tummy and made an alderman's thumb-ring shape with her fingers. She held that gesture high above her head for Olivia's class. Her cushion was slipping and she hurriedly replaced her hand on it, hiked it up and continued: 'A plague of sighing and grief, it blows a man up like a bladder.' The cushion was safely secured. She grew confident, and at the word 'bladder' she caressed her paunch and smiled confidently at Olivia's class. Her pals in there gave her a thumbs up. The bell rang before they were quite finished.

'Fantastic, girls. Well done,' said Olivia.

'Excellent, girls,' said Nell. 'Now when Mr Keogh comes in here after lunch, there is not to be a trace of a tavern, tankards or costumes. Right?'

'Right, Miss Hynes.'

'Will we be doing it in the hall, Miss Hynes?'

'I haven't made up my mind yet. That was very good but I'll discuss it with Mrs Colleran over lunch. Now remember, desks back in normal rows for after lunch. I'll be down to check.'

'Going to the staffroom for lunch, Nell?' asked Olivia.

'No, I've nothing in, Olivia. Anyway I want to get out of here for an hour.'

*

'Brown World by Nell Hynes.'

Nell typed her title slowly at the kitchen table. She had lots of A4 pages of *Brown World* written and she was anxious to type then up before the task grew too great. Then it would just be a matter of slipping them into a big brown envelope and sending them away to the publishers. Someone at the writing class, and she couldn't remember who, spoke of the 'slush pile' which was to be found in most publishing houses. Apparently this was the pile of manuscripts waiting to be read. These piles were rumoured to be very high. Nell hoped *Brown World* wouldn't languish too long in any publisher's slush pile. Her instinct told her it wouldn't, but then one could never be certain.

Nell typed on an old electric typewriter. Nearly all of Heather Connolly's students had PCs, but Nell was afraid to buy one, afraid that if she spent that much money it would cast a spell on her work. Better to wait at least until *Brown World* had been given some attention by a publisher. She didn't want to be like the really weak students in her own classes who had all the expensive student accessories. She was coming to the last hand-written page; the typing had familiarised her with the text. As she pounded the keys she marvelled once more at how good it was. *Brown World* was to be her secret – nobody she knew would hear of it until it burst on to the literary scene!

*I went out into Grafton Street. The cobbles were red and the sky was a dizzy June blue. That, at least, was reassuring. I still felt dreadful. My heart was racing and the butterflies still danced across my innards. It was shortly after eight o'clock. There were more pedestrians in the street now; two young men watered the hanging baskets and another swooped by me on a big machine with swirling brushes which swept the cobbles: Grafton Street was getting ready for another normal day. I took several deep breaths and decided to head for Stephen's Green. There I would sit and compose myself as best I could before heading for the office. I went through Fusileers' Arch and selected a seat in the shade by the duck pond. I fingered the inside of my wrist: my pulse was normal now and I began to feel a little better. What had that strange turn been about, though? I wondered. And while it was nearly gone, was it gone for good? If it had come upon me so unexpectedly couldn't it return just as unexpectedly? I took some more deep breaths. I felt exhausted and my day's work hadn't even begun. I got up from the seat and started to walk to my office.*

Nell reread the pages she had written. She wasn't at all pleased: they had no oomph she felt. They were leaden and dull. She wondered should she tear them up but decided against that. She would hang on to them, keep going – at least until better ideas came to her. If she didn't have any better ideas, they would have to do; not everything in this book could sing from the page with a high-octane intensity.

*I walked along Stephen's Green to my office. I work for the government; no more than that will I divulge to you, readers: my job isn't central to my tale. Suffice to say, it is dreary and tedious but I do it adequately, more than adequately. A few yards down the street, a voice called out my name. It was Stephen, my colleague and friend. Our paths crossed most mornings at this point and when they did we went the last few yards to the office together. Today, though, I dreaded our encounter. How could I cope with our customary badinage, the way I was feeling? Stephen too would surely notice something – he was uncommonly intuitive for a man. Stephen was at the door of the Shelbourne; I was across the street at the Wolfe Tone statue. There was nothing for it but to join him – he would be my litmus test for how I would cope with the world that day. I stepped from the footpath and into the street. A giddy sensation seized me. My foot seemed to need several minutes to reach the street; the street was slipping down and down as though it were subsiding. My foot hovered above the tar, dangling in the air, yet I couldn't bear to put it onto the street. It would be like stepping into a trough. The passers-by were crossing normally; Stephen was over there too, no doubt wondering what I was playing at. I closed my eyes and stepped forward. Everything was fine. One foot followed the other, and I joined Stephen at the Shelbourne. Was that giddiness connected to all the other bewildering feelings I had experienced that morning? I had no time to tease it out; I had to mask my terror and converse as normal with Stephen.*

A tiny bit better, thought Nell, as she read over the second chunk of *Brown World*. Some aspects of the style in this passage pleased her: she liked the reference to masking her true feelings, and the idea that her heroine worked for the government was good too. Literature was peopled with unimportant clerks toiling away in anonymous bureaucracies. And the reference to Stephen's intuition would surely score her some brownie points with the feminists.

But *Brown World* still wasn't flowing from her pen as it had on the first night, and that was upsetting Nell. She made some tea, selected a fresh page and sat back at the table. 'Whither *Brown World*?' she wrote. That seemed to be all she could come up with. There were hours and hours of good working time left before bedtime. She should be writing at a cracking pace, but nothing would come. There was nothing for it but to abandon it for the moment. She would do as Heather Connolly always advised: carry a notebook – maybe something might come to her as she went about her day's routine in school the next day. She knew she didn't have any unused notebooks in the house and decided straight away to go to Rathmines and buy a selection of nice notebooks. She would walk too; the stroll into Rathmines might loosen up whatever was blocking her creativity. She might even call in somewhere for a cappuccino – famous writers usually spent hours in coffee houses in European capitals, scribbling into their notebooks. She went to get her coat. She would have to walk smartly – the shops would be closing at six o'clock

Nell sat in an alcove in the coffee shop. She was almost hidden by the large potted palm. She stirred the frothy cappuccino and took a little sip and opened the bag from the stationer's shop. She pulled out two lovely notebooks – large, hardbacked, with marble-effect covers. They could fit into any pocket or handbag. One was for *Brown World* and the second would do for ideas she might get about Sir Bashel when she brought him back to life. She looked around the coffee shop. Several young people were actually writing. She peeped through the leaves of the potted palm. The young man opposite her was rolling a cigarette; several pages were on the table, each filled with small writing. Nell took the top off her fountain pen. 'Whither *Brown World*?' she wrote again. She stopped; she couldn't think of anything else. The young man resumed his work. Nell felt dispirited. How could he scribble away with such ease when she couldn't even write a syllable?

She turned to her second notebook. 'Sir Bashel?' she wrote. Casting her mind back some days, she recalled what she had written of that story and jotted it down in point form. She could expand on the points at home. *Brown World* would have to go on the back boiler until the muse alighted on her shoulder again. Meanwhile, she would pound out a few chunks of Sir Bashel. At least she would have her assignment ready for Heather Connolly's class. Nell drained the cup and ordered a second. I deserve a treat, she thought. It's not easy coming to terms with artistic frustration!

*

Nell had cleared away the dinner dishes and set up the kitchen table for a few hours of creativity. She opened her Sir Bashel notebook and transferred what she had written to some new pages. Soon she had her old story back again, intact. Barney, Isabella and Lady Montefiore were all there in front of her. Why, she wondered, did she always think of that story as the Sir Bashel story? She had actually stopped writing it before Sir Bashel appeared at all. It was like Hamlet without the prince. Introduce Sir Bashel; that's what she would do in order to flesh out the story a bit for the writing class.

*'Are you the English girl for Sir Bashel's place?'*

*Isabella had been lost in her own thoughts. She looked in the direction of the voice. A tiny man had spoken to her; he carried a whip, he was unshaven and his teeth were ugly, black stumps. That he was ugly and dirty didn't surprise her in the least. Everything about Ireland so far had been filthy and ugly. It was growing dusky. She had been travelling for almost two days, and she was tired.*

*'And who might you be, my man?' she asked.*

*'I'm Thady, Sir Bashel's man. I was sent to get yeh. Have yeh many portmantoes?'*

*Isabella could scarcely make out what the oaf was saying, but she nodded to her luggage, which was at her feet.*

*'Is it far?'*

*'About four mile. 'Twill be dark, though, when we get there.'*

*Thady loaded her luggage into Sir Bashel's carriage. Isabella stepped in herself – she couldn't bear to be handed in by Thady.*

*The carriage turned in the village square. Filthy, barefooted children played in the tiny street, and pigs and hens scavenged in gutters. It was all too incredibly horrible to contemplate. The hedges were high. The road the carriage took was little more than a lane; it was full of holes and the carriage lurched wildly. She felt ill. The filthy slop she had been served in the inn in Kinvara churned about in her stomach. She should never have accepted it.*

*The carriage stopped, and she heard gates opening, Thady*

threw the carriage door open. 'Well, yer landed, Miss. Let yeh hop down now and go into the kitchen. Bridie'll look afther yeh. I'll folley yeh with yer portmantoes.'

Isabella's eyes stung when she entered the kitchen. Whatever they burned in the fire, it wasn't coal. Her eyes streamed tears, acrid tears. The room was smoky and it stank; surely she couldn't be expected to eat what was prepared in this vile kitchen. Two crones stood by the fire: one stirred a large cauldron, the other turned a large flitch of meat on a spit. Their tasks completed, they resumed their seats on stools. Isabella stared at them in disbelief – they were actually smoking clay pipes!

'I am the new governess,' she began.

'Sure 'tis well we know it,' laughed one of the crones. She addressed her sister in a tongue strange to Isabella's ears. Good God, she thought, it must be Gaelic.

'There isn't many in these parts talk like that. Sure who else would ye be but the governess.'

Thady threw Isabella's luggage on to the kitchen floor. A terrible screech accompanied the thud of her luggage, and two white hens fluttered out from under the kitchen table.

'Thady, will yeh go aisy,' admonished the senior crone. She put down her clay pipe, wiped her hands on her apron and got up. 'Come on,' she said to Isabella, 'the masther and misthress are above in the parlour. They're expectin' yeh; I'll show yeh the way.'

When Isabella left the filthy kitchen, she noted with some pleasure that the rest of the house did bear a resemblance to a fine gentleman's residence. Her spirits lifted a little. Maybe her own apartments might even be tolerable. She climbed the stairs to the drawing room. Bridie knocked at the door. Without waiting to be asked to enter, she opened it roughly herself and shoved Isabella in ahead of her. 'Well, Mam, here she is, and a fright to God she is entirely.'

The Lady Oonagh Glockamorrah sat by the fire, and two great Irish wolfhounds slumbered before the embers. They each opened an eye, looked at Isabella and decided against devouring her. The Lady Oonagh had a pleasing countenance, and a full bosom. 'You are very welcome to Burren Castle,' she said. 'Please be seated.' Isabella sat and the Lady Oonagh addressed her. 'It appears that your little indiscretion is to be our gain,' she began. Isabella started. What had her mother communicated to the Lady Oonagh, she wondered.

'Don't flinch so, Miss Montefiore. Your mother's letter was tact itself. It is I who am reading between the lines. It is hardly customary for a daughter of one of the finest families in England to take up a position in what's little better than domestic service. But no matter, it was fortuitous. Sir Bashel and I had been seeking a governess for our sons. I wish them to be educated in England. When they have finished with you we will be sending them to Eton. It is essential that they go to boarding school; they need a man's hand. Sir Bashel, alas, is no longer in a position to play a father's role in his sons' lives.'

Isabella became aware of a strange gurgling sound. It did not come from the dogs; they were still sleeping contentedly before the fire. She looked around the room as best she could. Down at the end in the farthest corner sat a small, male figure. He was in a bath chair and a rug covered his knees.

'Sir Bashel O'Dell,' said the Lady Oonagh. 'My husband, your master, though of course all your dealings will be with me.'

Isabella scarcely knew what to say. She merely nodded. The tiny figure in the bath chair was little more than an imbecile. He writhed and twisted in his chair and made more gurgling sounds.

'A hunting accident,' said Lady Oonagh. She tugged at the bell rope beside the mantelpiece and Thady appeared.

*'It's time for Sir Bashel to retire,' she said. 'And when you have seen to Sir Bashel, bring some refreshments for Miss Montfieore.'*

*Though Thady was small, he lifted Sir Bashel with ease from the chair. He carried him to the door. Isabella saw him closely for the first time. He had such terrible eyes; they unnerved her completely. Though the body was wasted, the man's brain was still alive, very much alive. Isabella did not like what she saw.*

Nell had a big pile of pages on the table, all covered with the tale of Sir Bashel. The evening had flown by and it had been very productive: too productive, Nell felt. She was dismayed by the ease with which the Sir Bashel tale flowed from her pen. The implications for her writing career were not lost on her. *Brown World*, or any substantial literary work, was eluding her, yet the pages from the popular fiction work were stacking up ominously. She went to the dresser and poured herself a stiff home measure of Scotch. Sir Bashel's story would be a success, she felt it in her bones. It would make money, but she would be sneered at by the critics, ignored by the Arts Council. It would be nice to have money, have a current account in the black, but secretly she dreamed of artistic acclaim. She could bear the notion of slipping from favour for a short period after her death, but she couldn't countenance the idea that lasting posthumous acclaim might not be her destiny! And Sir Bashel O'Dell wouldn't bring Nell Hynes literary acclaim.

# CHAPTER SIX

'Oh, they have tiramisu,' gushed Miriam, 'and banoffee,' she continued. The trattoria's menu was on a laminated A3 page. Nell couldn't see Miriam's face behind it. 'You must have some tiramisu, Nell, it's divine.' The menu made a 'whock' sound as Miriam arranged it before her.

'Any ideas about main courses, Miriam?' asked Nell. Nell had her menu propped against her chest and she wasn't reading it.

'Main courses? I haven't even looked at the main courses yet,' she said. 'I've made you tiramisu, Nell, haven't I?'

'No,' said Nell.

'I have,' Miriam insisted.

'It must have been someone else. I only ate tiramisu once and it was in a restaurant.'

'You sure?'

'Yes.'

'Have you decided?'

'Yes, I am going to have the vegetarian pizza.'

Miriam came out from behind the menu for a moment and looked at the other tables. Waiters were carrying pizzas to these tables.

'Oh,' she gasped, 'I couldn't possibly go a full pizza. They look huge, unless of course you would share it with me?'

'No,' said Nell, 'I would like a full pizza myself.'

Miriam went back in behind her menu. 'I was sure you had tiramisu in my place, Nell,' she said absent-mindedly. Nell put her menu down on the table and rested her arms on it. A waiter approached. 'Ladies,' he said, 'are you ready to order?' Nell arched her eyebrows across at Miriam.

'Could you give us a few more minutes?' Miriam said to him. 'Nell, I can't make up my mind. Can you help? You come here all the time.'

'I have only ever eaten the vegetarian pizza here.'

'Yes, but they look huge. I would want to have been ploughing a field before I could tackle one of them. I had a scone after swimming and I still feel stuffed.'

'Still swimming, then?'

'Oh yes, I love it.' She smiled at Nell over the top of the menu. Nell could see the imprints of the goggles around her eyes. She gave her a little smile back.

'Hungry, Nell?' she asked.

'Very,' said Nell.

'You didn't have any lunch?'

'No, I was meeting you for lunch. Why would I have had lunch?'

'True,' Miriam laughed. 'You must be starving, so. You haven't eaten since breakfast.'

'Mmmm.'

'It's just that scone. I shouldn't have had that scone, and all these pasta things are so filling, and I don't even know if they're good here or not. Maybe if I just have a starter portion from the pasta menu and then I might just be able to sample their tiramisu, though if I do, Nell, you will have to help me.'

'I don't like tiramisu, Miriam.'

'I was sure you liked tiramisu, Nell.'

'Don't.'

'Did I not give you my tiramisu recipe, Nell?'

'No.'

'Who was it then?'

'No idea.'

'Wonder was it Rachel and Paul?'

'Probably.'

'No,' said Miriam, and she emerged again from behind her menu. 'It was Stephanie and Niall. I gave Stephanie the recipe. Now I remember. Were you not there that night, Nell?'

'No.'

'I was sure you were there that night. God I hate when these waiters don't give you time to look at the menu properly,' she said, as she saw the waiter approach their table again.

'I'll have a starter portion of lasagne with a green salad.'

'For you, madam?'

'Vegetarian pizza,' said Nell.

'And to drink?' asked the waiter.

'What's the house white like?' asked Miriam. 'Not too dry?'

'No, madam, not too dry.'

'Right so,' said Miriam, 'I'll have a glass of your house white.'

'And for you, madam?'

'Could you just bring me a jug of water please?' asked Nell.

'Certainly, madam.' The waiter took the menus and left.

'So,' said Nell. 'How are you, Mir?'

'Great, Nell, really great. Well work is the same as ever, that doesn't improve, but I feel better in myself.

When did we last meet?'

'August.'

'Right, August. Are you sure?'

Nell's stomach tightened. How could she not be sure? It was the day she had left for that holiday with Hugh when he had told he it was all over, that he had met somebody else. Didn't mean to hurt her, blah, blah, blah. Nell hadn't waited for his explanations. She had hired a car and gone straight back to Dublin – determined not to wait around for the 'at least let's be friends' routine. Of course she remembered when she had last seen Miriam.

'Yes, you were just back from Crete and I was going to Galway for the month.'

'Right, right.'

The waiter popped the glass of house white in front of Miriam and the jug of water in front of Nell.

'Nell, are you not drinking?'

'I'm going to the theatre tonight. I want to wait and have a drink then.'

'God, Nell, you're fantastic. I haven't been to the theatre in ages. This course just eats into all my time. I never get to see anybody from the old crowd. What's on?

'*Hedda*,' replied Nell.

'Come again.'

'*Hedda Gabler,*' said Nell.

'I think I heard something about that on the radio one evening; supposed to be brilliant, isn't it?'

'It's incredible. This is actually my second time seeing it. It's that good I don't mind going again.'

'That's something I really miss with this course – all those theatre evenings with you and Barbara and all the old crowd. Is that who you're going with?'

'Well, I'm not really sure who is going. Olivia asked

me when someone cried off. She knows I saw it but could go again. Olivia, obviously, is going, and Niall and Barbara and Conor, of course . . . '

'Barbara, gosh, Barbara, now there's a blast from the past. Is Barbara still with Conor?'

'Yes.'

'Anyone else?'

'Yes, some friends of Niall Colleran. I'm not sure really, but I'm really looking forward to it. The play is wonderful anyway, but this production is amazing.'

'I must really start going to the theatre again. I really miss it. It's just impossible to get the time.'

'Bound to be, Mir. Tell me about the course. I know you've told me but I get mixed up in all the details of courses friends are taking.'

The waiter arrived with the food. 'Green salad and starter portion of lasagne?' Nell nodded to Miriam.

'Will you really eat all that?' asked Miriam when she saw Nell's pizza.

'Remember, Mir,' said Nell, 'I didn't have a scone and I'm not cooking tonight and I was working all morning.'

'Working, on a Saturday?'

'It's a long story; I'll tell you later. Tell me about your course first.'

'It's called *ashoomi*.'

'Sounds Japanese.'

'It is. It's the ancient art of Japanese healing and massage.'

'But Miriam, I thought your course was something to do with Celtic spirituality.'

'Yes, Nell. What brought me to *ashoomi* was Celtic spirituality. The Celts originated in Japan; they were Oriental as well as Occidental.'

'Were they?'

'They were. Remember the first course I took? That was trying to get us focused on our Celtic roots, to explore what we lost when Christianity drummed all the Celtic stuff out of us. Are you interested in Celtic spirituality at all, Nell? Because if you are, there are some great books I could loan you.'

'No, Miriam, the Celts don't really do much for me. I think they are very overrated at the moment.'

'But that's just where you're wrong. Celtic spirituality teaches us so much about where we have gone wrong in the world today. If we could all just get in touch with our Cetic roots again, all that's wrong with the world today could be put to rights. See, Nell, when I was in my goddess group . . . '

'Goddess group? Miriam, I thought all this began when you took a course in Celtic spirituality.'

'It did, Nell, but after the spirituality course there were advanced spirituality courses and I took them. That led to the forming of a goddess group. Now, in my goddess group we were all trying to get in touch with the goddess within ourselves . . . '

'So, Miriam, are you a goddesss now or what?'

'See, Nell, this is the point: all women are goddesses. We all have the potential to exist as goddesses. In Celtic times all women were goddesses; there was no such thing as patriarchy.'

'Miriam, are men now gods in this Celtic mindset of yours?'

'Nell, you are just being cynical.'

'I'm not, Miriam, honestly I'm not. I'm just a little bit confused, that's all.'

'Of course men aren't gods. Celtic spirituality doesn't

empower men at all. It actually disempowers them, or rather wrests the power which they have from them and restores it to women – all perfectly fair and just in my view, since it was women's power in the first place. God, you're really getting through that pizza, aren't you?'

'Told you I would. I was starving.'

'I'm stuffed after that green salad. I don't think I could manage the lasagne.'

'Now, when did you get involved in all the Japanese massage and healing?'

'When I joined the goddess group our studies brought us to the teachings of Japanese philosophers, who, it turns out, all had their theories rooted in Celtic spirituality. I mean the influence of Celtic spirituality was so profound, so far-reaching, that it actually spread to Japan. The Japanese had a healing and massage system which was borrowed directly from the Celts. That's the *ashoomi* which I'm studying.'

'Miriam, is all this very time-consuming?'

'Just two nights a week, but then there's the meditation and studying and oh of course seeing clients – that takes a few hours a week, so yeah, I suppose it is, Nell. No wonder I haven't been to the theatre or seen any of the old crowd, but, Nell, it's worth it. I just feel so well.'

'That's great, Miriam, honestly. I'm really delighted for you. I was very glad to get your message on my machine last week, and now that you've explained what a goddess's schedule entails, not to speak of a trainee *ashoomi* therapist, I'm just glad you could find the time to call. No doubt the telephone must seem almost off-limits to a goddess.'

'Nell, I sense a great hostility in you. Maybe you could do with some *ashoomi*. It releases all the tensions and toxins which just build up.'

'No, Miriam, no anger at all; just making the point that nobody had seen you for a very long time – you've been missed.'

'Yes, but I've been working on myself, and that takes such time. I had such layers of bad stuff to strip away, and I still have so much more stuff to work through.'

'How long more until you qualify as an *ashoomi* therapist?'

'About eighteen months, not counting internship.'

'Internship?'

'Yes, I have to intern in a *sindra*.'

'A *sindra*?'

'A *sindra*, Nell. I'm sorry. Sometimes I forget when I'm talking to one of the old crowd or one of the uninitiated that the *ashoomi* terms are not just everyday parlance. A Sindra is an *ashoomi* centre of higher learning. Therapists intern there at the feet of the *ashoomi* masters for eighteen months before they can be deemed fit to practise as recognised *ashoomi* therapists. After internship I intend packing in teaching and practising as a full-time *ashoomi* therapist and healer. There now, half the lasagne, that is really all I can eat. Now, where is that waiter? We couldn't get rid of him earlier, now he's nowhere to be seen.' Miriam raised her hand and called the waiter. 'Some tiramisu and another glass of the house white,' she said.

'And you, madam?'

'Nothing, thanks,' said Nell. She raised her glass to Miriam. 'Cheers. I hope it all works out.'

'Thanks. So what was it that had you working this morning, Nell?'

'Writing. I'm taking a creative-writing class and I try to do a little bit each day.'

'Nell, isn't writing a bit cerebral? Why not do something like *ashoomi*, something a little more nuturing, some form of healing perhaps?'

'I don't feel the need to be healed, Miriam.'

'But Nell, we all need healing and nurturing. We're all wounded and hurting. What can writing give you?'

'I have no idea. It's just something I would like to try.'

'Want to taste some tiramisu?'

'I can't stand tiramisu.'

'Can't you? I was always sure you loved it. This is nice, but not as nice as mine.'

'Actually, Miriam, if you don't mind, I'm going to have to go. It's nearly three o'clock and I'd like to say a quick hello to my mother before I go out tonight. This should take care of my half.' Nell put a tenner on the table.

'Nell, you're too attached to your family; you allow them to make too many demands on you. If you did some work on yourself you could cut some of those ties.'

'I'll bear it in mind, Miriam. Take care.'

Nell left the trattoria and went to her car. She didn't drive away immediately. She sat and thought. She had left the trattoria abruptly and she knew it. But she had to. Going to see her mother was just an excuse to get out of the trattoria, away from Miriam. She was cross but she couldn't exactly work out for herself why she was cross. One thing she knew was that the two-hour lunch had been a waste of precious weekend time, time which would have been better spent working on *Brown World*. Even working on Sir Bashel O'Dell and his capers would have been more fruitful than listening to Miriam and her bloody tiramisu. She promised herself not to get in touch with Miriam again. She knew Miriam wouldn't be in touch; the goddesses would have prior claim on her time.

*

Nell went into the kitchen and plugged in the kettle. She switched on the radio and switched it off again – three solid hours of sport on Saturday wasn't to her liking. On the table was a full basket of ironing. She emptied the basket's contents on to the table, poured a cup of tea and began to fill the basket again with the clothes which didn't need ironing. She had only yanked them off the line that morning as she had run out the door to meet Miriam. The basket was now half-full and looked less intimidating. Finishing her tea, she opened the ironing board and started on next week's school blouses. She stretched the back of the blouse along the ironing board, squirted a little water on it and off she went, up and down in long even strokes and into the snaggy bits at the shoulders.

She thought about Miriam as she worked. Had she changed or was it Nell who had changed? She turned the blouse over, squirted again and nosed her iron in between all the buttons. Miriam had never been self-absorbed; they had always had long, serious conversations, funny ones too. She smiled as she recalled some of their dafter exchanges. Nell slipped the buttonless side on to the board; the room was filling with the smell of fresh ironing. Our conversations were never one-sided, either. I hardly got a word in edgeways this time. Though there was one good side to all her self-absorption: she had never mentioned Hugh. She probably thinks he is still here! Nell selected a sleeve and smoothed it out from the seam across the width of the board, replaying the conversation in the trattoria in her head. Bloody *ashoomi*, Celtic spirituality and tiramisu. What had happened to the woman's head since the goddesses had kidnapped her? Couldn't she see the irony of embracing a new, life-enhancing philosophy devoted to healing and nurturing whilst abandoning her friends? And what was all that rubbish about being stuffed after a green salad and a scone? The woman had just done millions of lengths of a pool, enough to burn off a dozen scones. And if she had become obsessive about weight, why go on and on about a dessert? Nell slipped the shirt on to a hanger. That looks nice, she thought. Might even give it a squirt of starch later.

She took another and continued. It was mean thinking nasty thoughts about a friend of long standing. You're not mean, though. Look at all these tiramisu evenings she appears to have had and you weren't invited, and she couldn't even remember whether you were there or not. She was careless with my feelings, Nell concluded, and I don't take that lightly. She was sending me messages all the time that I don't matter any more; she can't remember what I like to eat, she thinks I eat too much, I need to work on myself, get rid of my anger, not do a cerebral writing course. A sickening feeling gnawed at Nell's stomach. She stopped ironing and stood the iron on its end. She felt giddy. She touched the teapot. Damn! It was cold. She plugged in the kettle and made some more. She needed to think. Sitting at the table she held her mug with both hands; she felt shaky and a little bit cold. Nasty little truths were trying to dawn.

Stupid, that's what I am, she thought. How could I not see what she was at? Thought you were really smart with your little jibe about the phone, didn't you? Leaving the restaurant early was terribly assertive, you were really in control then, weren't you? You stupid, stupid woman. When will you ever learn? She was controlling you all the time and you couldn't see it. And what's worse, somewhere in that silly brain of yours, when her conversation was at its most infuriating, you thought that you might file bits of it away and use it some time in a bit of dialogue-satire, of course! Revenge is a dish best eaten cold and all that rubbish. Come on, admit it. When you stopped at the lights in Rathmines in clouds of high dudgeon you whispered in the car, she 'fears the lancet of my art'.

'Well, Nell Hynes,' she said aloud in the quiet kitchen, 'the laugh was on you.'

*

'Nell. Brian and Con, two friends of mine from work,' said Niall Colleran in the foyer of the Abbey Theatre. 'Nell works with Olivia.' Nell shook hands with the two men; she could see Barbara and Conor coming through the swing doors as she said hello. Barbara was beaming and she gave one of her fingery little waves to the group. The foyer was filling up. The aroma of coffee wafted across it, and it mingled with the scents of aftershaves and perfumes and the buzz of conversations.

'That's new, isn't it?' asked Niall. 'I mean, they don't usually do that here, do they?'

'It is. In fact it wasn't here at the start of the run,' said Nell. There was a huge still of Hedda above the door of the auditorium; it was from a point late in the play when Hedda was in mourning.

'It's very dramatic,' said Con, and they filed in to take their seats. Nell sat in the aisle seat; she wouldn't have to tip the seat up and let people squeeze past her. Their row was full. She looked at the set. It had taken her breath away when she had seen it the first time. It was Hedda and Jurgen Tessman's drawing room. A drawing room wasn't of its very nature anything spectacular to see on stage, but Nell had never seen the illusion of space captured so effectively before. The doors leading from the drawing room were enormously high; so too was the French door to the garden, which was still covered by a muslin curtain. Nell closed her eyes for a moment. She could still hear the crack of gunfire from Hedda's pistols as she fired through the curtain at the repulsive and predatory Judge Brack, and she remembered how the morning's early sun had glowed through the billowing muslin and the crows or rooks had cawed in the garden beyond it.

'You look fantastic,' Barbara whispered to Nell.

'Thanks,' said Nell. 'I did make an extra special effort.'

'Any particular reason?'

'I felt lousy. I wanted to cheer myself up. You know me, Barbara. I slap on lots of Elizabeth Arden's Flawless Finish if I feel down in the dumps; only tonight I had to make do with Max Factor Sheer Genius.'

'What happened?'

'Miriam is a bitch and I am a fool. The latter is much more painful than the first; sshhhh, I'll tell you later.'

It was a little before dawn; a figure in a nightdress paced the drawing room in an agitated state. The stage was lit in a pale greyish light, and as the figure roamed through the room she babbled incoherently. The figure in the nightdress was Hedda. After a few seconds she left the stage, and the drama of the marriage of Hedda Gabler to Jurgen Tessman began again – the drama of a newly-wed, ill-matched pair, just returned from the six-month wedding journey. Dull, dull Jurgen; fiery, crazy, doomed Hedda. Nell sat back, ready to be transported for a second time.

*

'Why did she marry Jurgen? Surely she must have known it couldn't work. Even Judge Brack would have been better – he had some idea of what made her tick.'

'Niall,' said Olivia, 'Judge Brack wouldn't have offered Hedda anything except the chance to be his mistress.'

'Pint of stout please, Conor,' said Nell. 'Gin and tonic,' said Barbara. Nell had positioned herself under Brian Friel's portrait beside Niall's friend Con. 'But surely,' said Con, 'it would be preferable to be the judge's mistress than to be married to Jurgen. She shrank every time Jurgen came near her.'

'But Hedda is conventional, too conventional to face the social censure a mistress would face.'

'Conventional?' shrieked Brian. 'She takes her pistols and fires out the French door at Judge Brack. She's a destructive bitch if you ask me – burning Loveborg's manuscript, goading him to drink too.'

'She is conventional and unconventional,' said Barbara. 'When Mrs Elvsted leaves her husband she is shocked; she knows what she will face from society.'

'What then if she hadn't married? She spoke of being General Gabler's daughter; she seems to have had some position in society. Surely she could have remained single?' wondered Niall.

'Being single wouldn't have been an option for her. Look at how she treated Jurgen's silly maiden aunts,' said Olivia and Barbara in a chorus.

'Yes, but they are silly bores,' said Niall.

'True,' said Nell. 'But part of the reason they are seen as inconsequential is because they are not married. Hedda is a product of her society every bit as much as she is a free spirit. She knows full well that would have been her fate had she remained single.'

'Yes, Nell, but Tessman? Why marry Tessman, of all people?'

'All the other men just offered sex. Tessman proposed. She said it herself. Loveborg or the judge would be more suitable, but neither would offer more than flings – wonderful flings, maybe. Tessman offered a home, the status of marriage. She thinks she will mould him, or ignore him, create her own salon, but it takes too great a toll. Suicide was her only option.'

'Depressing,' said Con. 'Another drink, anyone?' he asked. 'Nell?'

'No thanks, Con. I've lots here, and anyway I'm driving.'

Barbara and Olivia came back from the toilet. 'Shove up there, Niall,' said Olivia, 'I want to talk to Nell. I gather the meeting with Miriam wasn't a success.' And Barbara squashed on to the seat as well.

'Shhh, don't say anything for a moment. I just want to watch something.'

'What, Nell, what?' both women asked, and they craned their necks around to see whatever it was which had caught Nell's attention. 'Don't do that,' she hissed. 'I'm keeping an eye on Hedda, Jurgen and Mrs Elvsted; they're just walking to the bar. I love seeing actors after a performance, looking ordinary, no make-up, wearing Levi's after all those magnificent dress suits and long dresses with bustles. Fiona Shaw is the most moving Hedda I have seen. Remember Glenda Jackson on telly when we were teenagers? Great, but this was more subtle. Her bitterness and despair were more understated, her cutting comments were almost asides, really; and then of course, we're older too . . . '

'Nell,' snapped Barbara, 'shut the fuck up about Hedda and Jurgen for a moment, will you? Tell us about Miriam.'

Nell's musings about the play were genuine, and though she pretended not to hear Barbara and Olivia clamouring for all the details of her lunch with Miriam, she could hear them full well. She was unsure whether she ought to let rip about Miriam to them. Was there any residual loyalty to Miriam left? She debated this as she pronounced on the play. No, she decided, Miriam was history. Miriam was dead: she would offer her up on a platter to her other friends in the form of a post-theatre funny story.

'Ladies,' said Nell, 'you are dear friends, dear friends of very long standing, but I refuse to allow you to drag this evening down to Miriam's level. Hedda is deeply moving tragedy; Miriam is mere burlesque.'

'Stop pissing about and tell us what happened. Are we ever going to see her again?'

'Never, my dears, never,' announced Nell theatrically. 'Miriam, I fear, is lost to us, lost to the entire Western world, gone from the Occident to the Orient. She is going to live in a Japanese monastery and study healing and massage. You will not be seeing her for frivolous things like lunch or coffee; she will have no time to cavort with shallow types like us. The only likelihood either of you two have of seeing her again is if you need a bit of healing.'

'Go on,' said Olivia and Barbara.

'I'm telling you, it's the truth. We've been jettisoned.'

'Niall,' said Olivia, 'Miriam's gone into a monastery. Nell's just been telling us.'

'But sure she doesn't believe in God,' he said.

'Niall,' said Nell. 'This is a post-God experience; this is the goddess calling!'

'I wonder would it be nice and peaceful there, Niall. No kids calling me at dawn on Saturday morning,' said Olivia wistfully. 'I could just work on myself.'

'Olivia, you would never stick the celibacy,' said Niall.

'Well,' said Nell, 'we don't know whether celibacy is compulsory or not. Miriam didn't say and I forgot to ask.'

'The devotees have to be celibate probably, but the masters are multi-polygamous,' salivated Conor. 'That's usually the way in those culty things.'

'Last orders now, ladies and gentlemen, please.'

'Anyone having another?' asked Conor.

'I will,' said Brian. 'Not for me,' said Nell. 'I want to get up early tomorrow.'

'Or us either; we've a babysitter to take home,' said Niall. Barbara and Conor stayed on for another drink. 'Are you in the Irish Life car park, Nell?' asked Olivia. 'Come on so; we will walk back together.

'I'll ring you, Nell,' said Barbara. I want to know how the class goes.'

'Night,' they all chorused, and Nell, Olivia and Niall walked down the stairs and into the street. Last-minute drinkers were pouring from the pub across the road and men were selling copies of the *Sunday Tribune* and the *Sunday Independent*.

'This is mine,' said Nell, when they got to the car park. She hugged Niall and Olivia and drove off. Town was coming to life as Nell drove home. Couples kissed in doorways and drunken men peed in the streets. She drove into Parliament Street. Temple Bar was hopping as she paused at the traffic lights. She turned right into Lord Edward Street and droved up past Christchurch, down into Nicholas Street, up to the canal and home. When she opened the hall door she could see the ironing board still open in the middle of the floor, the long white sleeves of her school blouse trailed across it. She plugged in the iron, finished the blouse and folded everything away. She went to the bathroom, removed her make-up and went to bed.

# CHAPTER SEVEN

*Stephen hadn't noticed anything strange about me that morning at all, and as we strolled along the street to our office we talked and joked as we usually did. I still felt dreadfully uneasy; my stomach was churning and my head ached. But if I had managed to pass myself off as normal with Stephen, might I not equally do so with the others at work? I sat at my desk and opened the file I had been working on all week. The typewritten lines did not swim before my eyes as the newspaper print had, and I settled down to what I hoped would be a normal day's work.*

Nell had a half-page of *Brown World* written, but she felt it had no spark. She had sat down straight after breakfast on Sunday morning, hadn't dilly-dallied reading the Sunday papers and had resolved not to listen to Andy O'Mahony either. Several hours that morning were going to be devoted to serious writing, and the best she could come up with so far was these watery old paragraphs. Artists had to suffer for their art; creating wasn't always easy, but this was ridiculous.

*When five o'clock came I left the office and walked towards the Rathmines bus stops. The streets were crowded, everyone was enjoying the summer sun. Pubs had placed tables out on the street and people drank their beers and coffees at the makeshift pavement cafés. Buskers played and street-theatre companies performed. I strolled into Grafton Street and thought I might sit awhile at a pub table and enjoy a coffee myself.*

*'A large cappuccino,' I said to the waiter, and I reached into my bag and pulled out the paperback murder mystery I had on loan from the library. I slipped into the story easily and stirred the chocolate into the coffee and started to sip. The sun was still very warm. I could smell the garlic from the restaurants in the street; it didn't seem like Dublin at all. I read some more pages. I don't particularly like murder mysteries but I always have one in my bag for reading over a solitary cup of coffee. And suddenly I felt it again, that horrible panicky feeling welling up in the pit of my stomach. Even though I was outdoors I felt as though I couldn't breathe. I had to leave, leave this place quickly; demons of some sort were in pursuit of me and all I knew was that if I kept on the move they couldn't keep up with me. I put some money on the table and walked off. I could not think of taking the bus home now. If I felt claustrophobic in the street, a bus in rush-hour traffic would be ten times worse. I decided to walk to Rathmines. I walked back up Grafton Street and into Stephen's Green, hoping and praying that I would not run into someone I knew. Strange noises were buzzing in my head and my ears were ringing. I felt very dizzy, but I kept on walking. I was like a mad thing, a creature possessed. And then the streetscape began to change. It didn't turn to brown as it had done that morning; it turned white: railings, streets, buildings, every single thing was white. I tried to talk myself out of my panic. 'This isn't happening,' I told myself. 'You are just hallucinating.' I put out my hand to steady myself against a railing in Harcourt Street and screamed because, although the railing was white like everything else, I hadn't expected the textures around me to alter as well. The railing didn't feel like metal; it felt soft, as though it were*

*padded. I squeezed it with my fingers. I was right. It was soft*
*and spongy to touch. I looked around me: all the bricks of the*
*Georgian houses in Harcourt Street had changed to the same*
*upholstered texture, and the street beneath my feet was springy*
*to walk on. Down Harcourt Street small, spongy white buses*
*and cars travelled, and little white, soft men, women and*
*children walked to and fro as though nothing were happening.*
*My whole world was turning into a gigantic padded cell, and*
*the worst of it all was that nobody had heard me scream.*

I like that, thought Nell. Now you are getting places. At
least she is hallucinating again. She's adrift in the world
and nobody knows how she is feeling – that could be a
metaphor for all sorts of things. It's up to the critics to
figure it out. She counted all her *Brown World* pages. There
weren't many, not nearly as many as Sir Bashel O'Dell,
but she was making some progress. Maybe it was no bad
thing that she had more Sir Bashel pages than *Brown
World* pages. She would be in real trouble artistically if
the work she firmly believed had something to say was
being written too easily. She lined the pages up neatly on
the table, drew her notebooks to her and sat down to
lunch. She would scribble down a few points for the next
stage of *Brown World* as she ate.

Nell went to the front of the notebook and tried to
think where she would bring *Brown World* to next.
'Relationships?' she wrote. The central character in her
novel had to be unmarried, she thought. I wouldn't know
how to write a realistic picture of married life. Better too
to keep her uninvolved romantically. If I'm trying to create
a sense of alienation and isolation she can't very well have
a satisfying sex life. Practical too: don't think I'd be the
best on writing sex scenes! 'Family?' Better leave them

out of it, too. I'd have to be writing dialogue all the time. It was looking like *Brown World* was going to be the slimmest of slim novellas at this rate. But, thought Nell, it doesn't have to be if I concentrate on my character's interior life.

Once Nell had those few guidelines noted, she closed her *Brown World* notebook. She knew exactly where she would pick up next time. Nell didn't mind turning to Sir Bashel now that she had accomplished something worthwhile. She opened her notebook and looked at her notes. Ah yes, I remember now, she thought, and she began to write.

*'The Lady Oonagh said I might come to the kitchen and get some hot milk for my bedtime cocoa,' said Isabella as she entered the smoky kitchen. Isabella was unprepared for the scene she saw: Thady, Bridie, Cissy and Steveneen the boots were kneeling on the floor with their arms resting on kitchen chairs. Thady was speaking aloud and the others were answering him. Then Cissy spoke aloud and the others answered her. Bridie motioned to Isabella to enter and wait a moment. She gestured to her that whatever they were doing was nearly finished. Although they all spoke quickly, Isabella was now growing accustomed to their thick brogues. She thought she could discern the words of prayers. Her observations were correct, for a few moments later the entire staff of Burren Castle blessed themselves and said a loud amen.*

*'Sorry to lave ye waitin', Miss Isabella, but we always say the Rosary before the cocoa. There's plenty a milk; take a seat a while sure and dhrink it with us. Pull over there to the fire.'*

*Bridie was being kind and Isabella realised it was no time for squeamishness. She had not spoken to a single human being all day; her three charges scarcely counted.*

'Thank you, Bridie,' she said. Bridie issued some kind of command to Steveneen and Cissy, who scuttled out of the kitchen and up the back stairs. She used the Gaelic again, Isabella supposed, for she couldn't understand a word.

'Well, are ye settlin' in, Miss Isabella?' asked Thady in between puffs of his pipe. Bridie picked up hers too and placed an ember on the top of its bowl. She sucked greedily on it and the tobacco reddened into life. She picked the ember from the bowl with the tongs and threw it back onto the fire. She poured Isabella a mug of cocoa and another one for Thady and herself.

'Yes, thank you. I have grown a little more used to Burren Castle and Ireland, I think, though I do miss my home and my family.'

'And the young lads, are they good scholars?' asked Thady. In truth, Isabella thought they were not in the least bit adept at their lessons; but it wouldn't do to gossip about the master and mistress's children to the servants in the kitchen.

'They are good scholars,' she lied.

'Oh, indeed and 'tisn't surprisin'. The O'Dells was always clever and the Glockamorrahs too, though I know less about them for they're from over Gort way.'

'Does the Lady Oonagh hunt still?'

'Hunt?' laughed Thady. 'Sure girl, nobody in this family ever went in for huntin'. There's hardly any huntin' in these parts. The nearest to here now for huntin' would be the Galway Blazers, and they're still a good few mile off. What put huntin' into your head at all?'

'Sure, Thady, maybe 'twas the lonesomeness did it, maybe ye did a bit of huntin' yerself beyant in England,' said Bridie.

'Yes, we all did. My father was master of the hunt for many years, but it wasn't that which made me ask. I merely wondered if the Lady Oonagh stopped hunting since Sir Bashel's accident. I have never seen any hounds at Burren

Castle and I wondered had they been got rid of.'

'Child, what are ye talkin' about at all. Sir Bashel never had any accident and we never had any hounds at Burren Castle.'

'But the Lady Oonagh told me that was why he was in a bath chair,' said Isabella. Bridie looked at Thady and they puffed at their pipes, saying nothing for a moment.

'So that's what the poor craythur told the girl. Well I suppose she had to say somethin' to put a bit of a face on things,' sighed Thady.

'Ah, sure ye wouldn't begrudge her that much,' said Bridie. 'Sure the poor thing got a terrible land entirely when she married Sir Bashel. She thought she would be the mistress of the finest place in Clare. What did she get instead but landed with a cripple. Sure the man is demented; he is not long for this world at all and twasn't any huntin' accident put him where he is today, I can tell ye.'

'What is the true story?' asked Isabella.

''Tisn't right to be talkin' about Sir Bashel to an outsider. Sure can't ye do yer work like a good girl and not be botherin' about what doesn't concern ye?'

'But Thady, it does concern the girl,' said Bridie. 'She's only a youngster, and a good-lookin' one at that. She needs to protect herself; sure I warned Cissy myself.'

'Well ye'd no right to be warnin' Cissy. Cissy's in no danger from Sir Bashel. 'Twas only ever gentry he went after.'

'But Thady, now that he is stuck in that ould chair, won't he take what he can get?'

Isabella was very unnerved by what she was hearing, but it explained why she felt uneasy in Sir Bashel's presence, and it accounted for his lingering looks and his unnerving eyes.

'Look, Thady, I don't care what ye think. Miss Isabella is only young, and she is far away from her family. I am goin' to tell her meself if you don't.'

'Right so, woman. I can see ye won't give me a moment's aise until I tell her.' He turned to Isabella. 'Miss Isabella, what I am goin' to tell ye isn't to go beyant these four walls. The Lady Oonagh must never know you know. She had her own reasons for not tellin' ye. I'm sure she didn't want it known over in England.'

'I assure you both I shall keep whatever you tell me in the strictest confidence.' Why couldn't the bumpkin get to the point quickly? If she were in some danger by being at Burren Castle she wanted to know immediately. She would communicate the matter post haste to her mother, and if it were serious enough maybe her mother might give her leave to return home. However much her mother and father were outraged by her indiscretion with Barney, they wouldn't want her to remain somewhere she might be in danger. Hope sprang in her bosom; she might have a way out yet!

'Miss Isabella, I'm sure 'tis the same with the gentry in England,' began Barney. 'The young men all have an eye for the ladies. They don't want to wait till they settle down and marry to enjoy ladies' company. Well, Sir Bashel was no different. He was a great ladies' man; he had women all over the place. He had women as far over as Kinvara; he even had wan for a while down in Ennistymon. Oh, he was a terror entirely.'

Thady sipped his cocoa and poked the fire. He was in no rush to complete his tale. 'And his father and uncles were always the same. Don't be too hard on poor ould Sir Bashel, Miss Isabella. He paid a very high price for his love of women, a very high price entirely.'

'Yerra, I've no sympathy for him at all. 'Tis the Lady Oonagh I feel sorry for. Sure he's no father to the children. For all we know she could be afflicted too. Wouldn't ye think he would have learned from watchin' his own father's end. And his uncles – sure ould Sir Bashel went the same way, and his uncle Cashel over in Dunguaire, and as for Dashel down in Inagh sure 'twas the very same. All of them, Miss Isabella, mad for women, all of them rotten with syphilis and cracked in the head from it. But not so cracked that they wouldn't make a lunge still at a poor girl that was handy. So mind what I'm sayin' te ye: keep well away from Sir Bashel.'

'And is there no cure?'

'None at all in the wide earthly world. We took him to doctors everywhere – Galway, even Dublin – there was nothin' any of them could do. 'Twould break yer heart to see him, babblin' away there like an amadán, and once he was one of the finest-lookin' men in these parts.'

'Is it known outside the family?'

'Sure 'tis the talk of the five parishes. Isn't there very bad blood between the Lady Oonagh's family over it? They didn't know Sir Bashel was ill when they were makin' the match. Sir Bashel couldn't leave the house for months when the secret came out. Lady Oonagh's brothers and fathers and uncles would have had him shot on sight. They were waitin' for him to appear. None of that matters now. They may make all the fuss they like over gettin' back the dowry, for the poor craythur can hardly go from room to room without my help.'

'Is Sir Bashel mobile at all?'

'Oh, ye needn't worry, Miss Isabella, he won't come near ye. He hasn't walked for months.'

'Yes, but Thady, he could ask her to hand him somethin'. That's what he did to poor Cissy – asked her to hand him his pills and then he made a grab at her, tried to kiss and fondle her, she wasn't the better of it for days, so I'm warnin' ye, Miss. Don't go near him.'

'Ah, yer too hard on him, Bridie; have ye no pity?'

'Deed an I'm not, men are always too aisy on other men,

Miss Isabella. Finish up that cocoa now, Thady. 'Tis nearly midnight, and the tenants are comin' in the mornin' with the rent; we'll all be very busy.'

'Gracious,' said Isabella, 'I had no idea it was so late. Thank you both for your candour. I shall be the very soul of discretion – I give you both my word.'

'God bless ye, Miss. Yer not the worst. I had ye down for an awful madam entirely when I collected ye that day in the square, but sure once we got used te ye we could see ye were one of our own.'

Isabella left the kitchen. She was uneasy about Sir Bashel. Even though he was incapable of troubling her, his wicked past sickened her. Were all the gentry like that, as Thady claimed? Had her father pursued women until he became ill and could do so no more? Maybe the gout her mother claimed he suffered with was not gout at all. He was, however, quite lucid, and Sir Bashel, it was clear, was afflicted with some form of dementia. She went up to her bedroom, and as she climbed the stairs to her room she pondered on the injustice of it all: not Sir Bashel's position – nemesis was his portion – but she had been harshly treated. Her liaison with Barney had been pure and innocent but she had been banished. Sir Bashel's activities as a young man had been nothing short of depraved, yet she sensed a sneaking regard for him in Thady's voice as he told the story. How could she function as a governess to three little boys? She knew nothing at all. This evening had taught her more in less than an hour than she had learned from her books in all the years she had spent in the schoolroom with her own governess. She would write to her mother this very instant. It would need delicacy of phrasing and some artful planning so that Lady Montefiore would not think her plea to come home a mere ruse.

Nell had writer's cramp. She flexed her fingers; there were six A4 pages on the kitchen − eight pages all told if she included what she had written of *Brown World*. A very productive morning, she told herself. I'm not writing another word of Sir Bashel O'Dell until after the writing class. She already had almost a hundred pages; that was several chapters. The fact that she didn't have an outline of the whole novel didn't bother her. In truth she didn't know where the story was going. Moreover, she didn't especially care. Her productivity embarrassed her. That's it for today at the writing, she thought. She picked up her jacket and car keys. I'll go and see Mammy, she decided. As she got up to leave she turned back, picked up her Sir Bashel pages and brought them with her. Maybe Mammy might like to read a bit of Sir Bashel!

*

'Hand me my other glasses so,' said Mrs Hynes when Nell offered to show her mother Sir Bashel. 'I'd love to read it.'

'Pass me the pages as you finish,' said Nell's sister Patsy, who was visiting too. They pushed back the butter dish and the milk jug and spread Nell's pages out on the table and got stuck into the tale of Sir Bashel O'Dell.

'Where are you off to, Nell?' asked Mrs Hynes. 'Can't you stay here and explain it to us?'

'It shouldn't need any explaining. It's no good if it does. I'm going into the other room. I couldn't just sit here and watch you reading it,' said Nell.

Nell went into the sitting room and sat on the couch. The television was on but the sound was low. Nell turned it off. She looked out the French door to the garden. Her mother's bedding plants were still blooming; her own had long since fallen victim to the greenfly. Nell opened the door and went outside. She walked down to the back wall and looked up at the backs of their neighbours' houses. She could see nothing of the other gardens. Walls had been built and the trees and hedges had grown too high. As a child, Nell had been able to see right through all the gardens up to the top of the road and on and on as far as the Three Rock mountain. Her mother's garden might well now be in the heart of the countryside, for all they could see of the other houses.

These gardens had been noisy places when Nell was a child. Every family had had four or five children and they had flown around on bicycles or fought like cats and dogs over some toy. And whatever back garden they were in it didn't matter: on long summer nights there was always a window with the curtains drawn. The baby of the family still had an early bedtime, and when the baby became a tot he or she would climb out of bed, draw the curtains back and cry to join the big ones down in the garden playing. Nell and her friends would laugh up at the indignant little figures wailing as they crouched on the window ledges. They stuck their thumbs in their ears and 'nah nah nah nahed' up at them too. Mammies would bang on the kitchen windows if their games got too boistrous or if they went too near the washing lines. The washing lines were huge then: nappies cracked in the sharp breezes and men's shirts swelled and tumbled and twirled in amazing stunts. Nell's mother just had a rotary line now. The light was fading and Nell felt chilly. She decided to go back inside and see how Sir Bashel was being received.

'Now, can I get you a little bit of dinner, Nell?' asked her mother.

'No, I had my dinner, thanks.'

Patsy came through from the kitchen and sat on the couch beside Nell.

'Are you sure, Nell? There's lots left from my dinner.'

'Honestly, Mammy, I had a big dinner myself at home.'

'A drink, then?'

'Ah no, school tomorrow.'

'A drink would blot school out,' said Patsy. 'That's a very good idea.' And she went to the press and poured herself one.

'Sherry, Mammy?' she asked.

'Sure why not. But first I want to get Nell some tea. Maybe you'd have a few sandwiches with the tea, Nell?'

'Just tea, Mammy, honestly. I have eaten.'

'That's a shame. I have some lovely corned beef left and I could make it into sandwiches in a moment. Patsy had some and she thought it was nice, didn't you Patsy?'

'Mammy,' said Nell, 'sit down. I'll make my own tea. Drink your sherry and talk to Patsy.' Nell went to the kitchen and made a pot of tea. Her Sir Bashel pages were lying on the table.

'I made a pot and there are cups for everyone, so help yourselves,' she said, carrying in a tray. Now, Mammy, Patsy, did you read my story? What did you think?'

Mrs Hynes took off her reading glasses, put on her other glasses and sipped her sherry. 'Let me collect my thoughts,' she said.

'Ah, Ma, hurry up,' said Patsy, 'Well, if she won't get to the point quickly, I will. I think it's brilliant. I'm dying to know what happens next. Will Sir Bashel rape Isabella?'

'Patsy!' shrieked Mrs Hynes. 'That's enough. Nell wouldn't write about such things.'

'Course she would if there was money in it, wouldn't you, Nell?'

'I might if it were consistent with the artisic dictates of the storyline, yes. I can honestly say I wouldn't demur at including a rape scene.' Nell made a bold face at her mother and she and Patsy laughed. 'But,' said Nell, 'Patsy Hynes, you can't have been paying close attention to my text if you ask me whether Sir Bashel might rape Isabella. Surely you noticed my touching words about his almost complete incapacitation?'

'I know. I was just thinking that maybe he might gain a last little bit of strength in his death throes, make a lunge and just manage to pull it off.' Patsy lay back on the sofa, lost in lascivious thoughts.

'Now, Nell,' said Mrs Hynes, 'while she has paused for air, let me tell you I think it's wonderful. I was trying to think what it put me in mind of; it just came to me there when Patsy was talking, and it was the Irish RM. Do you remember the Irish RM? In fact, I think it's better than that.'

'Oh, Mammy's little pet,' sneered Patsy. 'Better than Somerville and Ross now. Well, I've heard everything. Nell, it's great, really it is. Is it a spoof, though, or is it for real? You don't read books like that, do you?'

'No, you're right, I don't, but it's not a spoof – or at least it's not meant to be. I wrote it because we got the assignment in the writing class and I wanted to write something completely removed from my own life.'

'And look what you did make up, Nell,' beamed Mrs Hynes. 'It's wonderful, that's what it is, wonderful. When I think of the rubbish that's published nowadays and the brass neck of some of the people who are writing. There was this one the other day on *The Arts Show* – you girls won't have heard it. Anyway this one had written a novel – apparently it's taking the place by storm – well, she read a bit of it and I declare to God, pussy would write better. It wasn't a patch on your story, Nell. Be sure now and finish it and ask that whatever her name is who's giving the class to give you the names of people you could send it to.'

'I wonder will she be reunited with Barney? Or will they ever allow her home to England?' Patsy mused. 'Should she forget all about him and maybe fall for someone in Ireland?' she continued. 'Nell, help me out here, I'm dying to know.'

'Patsy, I don't know myself.'

'You don't seem too enthusiastic either. You should care about your creations.'

'I don't care about this story at all, you're right. When I sat down to write I wanted to write something deep, something worthwhile. This is only a potboiler.'

'Yeah, but a potboiler which could prove to be a nice little earner,' said Patsy. 'Finish Sir Bashel, Nell, I'm dying to know what happens to him. I'd love a book like that to bring on my holidays.'

'But Patsy, I'm embarrassed to be associated with this kind of fiction – it's crap.'

'I wish to God you girls would mind your language,' said Mrs Hynes. 'Nell, this is not . . . what you said. It's a valuable piece of social commentary; the classes are wonderfully juxtaposed here. Look how you observe the servant class still speaking Irish and the English girl's belief that Thady, Bridie and Cissy are subhuman because they are Irish and servants. You two needn't be looking at me like that. That's the way they talk about books on the radio – books which aren't a quarter as good as yours,

Nell, so don't let me hear another word about . . . well, you know what.'

'Yes, Mammy, I'm listening. I won't kill Sir Bashel, I promise I won't.'

'You weren't really thinking of killing him off, were you?' asked Patsy.

'I was,' said Nell. 'And I may still kill him. He exists just for the writing class. I have no artistic loyalty to him,' she added in a whisper, for Patsy's ears only.

'Ah, please Nell, don't kill Sir Bashel, I beg you, spare his life,' Patsy laughed into her gin.

'Well, I might just condemn him to death and put him on death row; then you could write to him, Patsy,' laughed Nell.

'I hope you will remember all of us when you're rich and famous,' said Patsy. They got up from the couch and followed their mother to the kitchen. Mrs Hynes had a large plate of sandwiches in the centre of the table; she stood at the sink making tea in her biggest teapot.

'There's fruit cake too, Nell. Patsy, would you like some scones?'

'No thanks, Mammy, sandwiches are more than enough.'

'There's the rain now. The nights are really drawing in, aren't they?'

Nell smiled at Patsy. Mrs Hynes always commented on how long or how short the evenings were. 'Yes,' Nell replied. 'We're really back in full swing at school now.'

'Nell, I don't think you were here when I was telling Patsy; do you know who died?' There was never a visit to her mother which didn't include a reference to someone who had died. 'No, Mammy, I didn't hear,' she said. 'Who was it?'

'Poor old Ritchie Sweeney. You remember him, don't you?'

'Remember the Sweeneys?' squealed Patsy. 'How could we forget the Sweeneys, the perfect Sweeneys who got nine million honours in their Leaving Certs and first-class honours degrees – pains, the whole lot of them. I am sorry that the ould bloke is dead,' she added hastily. 'I never liked him, though. He'd never give us the ball back when it went into his garden and he wouldn't let Joe and Anna watch *Top of the Pops*; thought it was immoral. I told him you and Daddy watched it all the time and that you even danced together!'

'Patsy!' said Nell and Mrs Hynes together. 'You didn't.'

'I did so. I wasn't going to let that ould fellow think everyone was as narrow-minded as him.'

'Patsy, I can't believe you said that to him. All the times I said hello to him after Mass, all the serious conversations we had about politics. He would have thought I was dancing around at home with your father!'

'Do him good,' said Nell. 'What did he say when you told him, Patsy?'

'He said Mammy and Daddy should know better and it was no wonder we were all wild.'

'Is there anything else you'd like to tell me, Patsy?'

'How do you mean, Mammy?'

'She wants to go around to all the neighbours who you, aged five, made outlandish statements to, and deny them, but Mammy's in a hurry, Patsy. She has to get there before they pop their clogs. The penultimate knock on their doors will be Nancy Hynes setting the record straight. "It's only Nancy," she will say as she knocks on the door. "I am here to say that whatever my Patsy said about Enda and I having kinky sex in the rhubarb patch

when the children were gone to the procession is not true."
And the next knock at their door will be the man with
the hood and the scythe. Mammy, have some sense. It
was years ago, whatever that one told them I am sure
they don't even remember it.'

It was dark outside, and rain flecked the window-pane.
'You know Mammy, I'll have to be off soon,' said Nell.

'Me too, there'll be search parties out for me,' said
Patsy.

'Stay for *Glenroe*, Patsy,' said Mrs Hynes.

'Right, but the minute they play "dee dee dye dye diddle
dye ddee dye", I'm out of here.'

Nell finished her tea and got up to leave. 'Now don't
you stand outside waving,' said Nell to her mother. 'It's
chilly and it's spitting rain.'

They hugged and Nell got into her car, and her mother
stood in the doorway. The hall was dark but the kitchen
light shone from behind her. Nell thought her mother
looked small and frail. All the women on the road looked
like that now. The road was a road of widows; death had
been coming regularly, picking off the men one by one.
All the daddies were going – the nice ones and the not-
so-nice ones – and now poor Ritchie Sweeney. But the
women were wiry, made of sterner stuff; they were holding
on. Nell backed her car into the road. Before pointing it
homewards she gave a last wave to the small figure in the
doorway, and then she drove off.

# Chapter Eight

'My guests this evening are Constance, Maud and Imogen Hynes McAllister, names which at first will mean little to the listeners. These women are young, young enough to achieve greatness in their own right, but their current claim to fame is being the nieces of the acclaimed novelist Nell Hynes. In this programme, the second in the series 'Living With . . . ', where we talk to family members of the famous and try to discover what it must have been like to have known a famous person intimately, we continue our discussion with the nieces of one of the country's foremost novelists. So, Imogen, did you know, growing up, that your aunt was an important literary figure?'

'Not at all. She was just our aunt, one of my mother's sisters. My mother had four sisters. Nell was just one of them − we loved them all, but we had no sense that Nell was in any way different or unusual,' said Imogen.

'Was that in any way attributable to the fact that you grew up in a veritable artists' colony. Your mother is the watercolourist Patricia Hynes McAllister and your other aunt is the noted critic and academic Kate Hynes?'

'Not entirely,' said Maud. 'I think I know what Imogen means: all children accept the occupations of the adults they know as the norm. It makes no difference to the child whether the father is a painter or a coalman, but I take your point about creative families; ours was a creative family. Not to have been involved in some branch of the arts would have been commented on rather than the reverse, but I never thought that it was different in other families until I grew older.'

'Constance is smiling,' said the interviewer. 'What prompts you to smile, Constance?'

'Maud speaking about the family being creative. That's a rather anodyne term for it: it was a chaotic, undisciplined house. People called at all hours of the day and night; some came for dinner and ended up staying weeks. There was noise all the time, music playing – my parents and their friends loved dancing, which usually didn't begin until about midnight, and of course there were endless discussions about politics and art. For a time I hated it; I wanted to join a normal family, where the parents had nine-to-five jobs. Now I realise what a privilege it was to grow up in such an environment. Nell was part of that life, but she didn't stand out, because everyone was creating something.'

'From a child's perspective, what was Nell like?'

'Great fun,' chorused the three women. 'Interviewers usually view that with disbelief. I know that her novels are deeply serious, but honestly, she was, and still is, great fun,' continued Constance.

'She didn't play games with us in the garden or anything like that. She talked to us a lot, and when we were teenagers she was wonderful at keeping our secrets. Anything we told Nell never got back to my mother,' said Maud.

'Were you aware of her writing?'

'Yes, she spoke of it all the time. We asked her how her books were coming along, even though we didn't have a clue what they were about. We asked her in the same way she asked us about school.'

'When we were very young,' said Constance, 'Nell and my mother were still full-time teachers. My mother's painting career hadn't really taken off, and both Nell and my mother lived for the long school holidays, which freed up their time to do the work which really mattered to them. For ages I thought that Nell and my mother were two teachers who scribbled and painted in the holidays.'

'Were they close?'

'They have always been very close. My mother is the only woman I know who can talk for two hours on the phone to someone who will be visiting later in the day – that is how she and Nell communicate. When we were growing up and Nell would come to visit she always brought some pages of what she was working on for my mother to read,' said Imogen.

'And my mother would whisk Nell off to her studio the moment she arrived. She always showed her work to Nell before anyone else,' added Maud.

'Was there ever any artistic rivalry or jealousy?'

'Never. They were both very strong women, but sparks never flew about their art, possibly because they functioned in different spheres. Nell always claimed to know nothing of the visual arts, and while my mother read voraciously, she claimed to be unable to write a creative line. They supported each other generously without ever treading on the other's toes. Anyhow, their careers took off at about the same time: my mother had her first successful exhibition at the same time as *Brown World* was published,' said Constance.

'Were any of you aware of the impact *Brown World* made?'

'All I can remember,' said Imogen, 'is being allowed to stay up very late because Nell was going to be on the television. I thought that was very exciting and I remember boasting to my friends at school about it, but I fell asleep through the programme.'

'I can remember trying to read *Brown World* when it came out,' said Maud. 'I couldn't understand a word of it. I felt terrible. I wanted to say to Nell that it was great. Secretly, though, I thought it wasn't a patch on Enid Blyton.'

'Are there any disadvantages to being the nieces of one of the country's most revered novelists?'

'The most difficult thing to endure is the intrusions into the family's privacy,' said Imogen. 'Nell and my mother have suffered horribly from that. It's not like the papparazzi are after Nell or our mother, but the endless stream of thesis research students and queries from scholars who are doing this paper for that summer school or this journal are the most trying, particularly for our mother, for, as you know, Nell is especially adept at eluding these people.'

'Yes,' said the interviewer, 'and she probably escapes the brunt of them as she spends so much time now in Tuscany. Now correct me if I'm wrong, but I read somewhere that Nell and the whole family were especially distressed by the Lionel Sears biography. How can that be, when it was hailed as one of the most outstanding biographies of recent times?'

'Lionel Sears is a noted scholar of Irish literature. His credentials are certainly impeccable. Nell was in Tuscany when Sears came to Dublin, and she refused to return to meet with him; she wasn't going either to cooperate with him or block him. Nell was quite happy for our mother to work with him,' explained Constance, 'but what she wasn't prepared for was his slant on Nell's life. That distressed all of us. My mother had no idea he was into all that Freudian Jungian psychoanalytical . . . can I say "shit" on family radio? Well, there, I've said it, that's what nearly did my poor mother in.'

'The revelations about Nell's sexuality . . . ?'

'Speculations, corrected Maud. 'Yes, they were terribly painful. All that wonderful creativity after *Brown World* being attributed to her passionate liaisons with three key women in her life. We knew these women; they were her friends, nothing more. My mother suffered hours of anguish over what she might have unleashed by co-operating with Sears. She bitterly regretted not having listened to Muriel . . . '

'Muriel?' asked the interviewer.

'Yes,' said Maud, 'Muriel Spark. She was Nell's neighbour in Italy when Nell first began to winter there. Muriel telephoned my mother to warn her about co-operating with Lionel Sears. She told our mother not to let him near Nell's life. He would do a hatchet job, she said. She tried to warn Nell, but Nell was too engrossed in writing *Little Treasons* to listen. And she had Iseult Campbell staying too, at the time, so I suppose she just wanted to enjoy her company and get on with the book. Anyway, Muriel was getting on a bit by then, and if Nell wasn't unduly perturbed by Sears, my mother thought it all right to proceed with working with him.'

*

'Ouch,' said Nell. Her elbow slipped from the table edge and her arm crashed to the kitchen table with a heavy thud. She had been supporting her cheek with her arm and her face hit the table too with a nasty smack. A loud, insistent knocking at the hall door had brought her reverie to an end.

She stood up, slightly dazed, and went to answer the door. Two beautiful men stood on her step. Nell's stomach tightened: one of the men was the image of Hugh. 'Of course we will always be friends, won't we, Nell?' Hugh's words played themselves once more in Nell's head, and she looked at the man. His lips were moving.

'Good morning, ma'am,' he said. His eyes were dark blue.

'Isn't it a lovely morning, ma'am?' said the other one. Nell nodded weakly.

'Can we interest you in the words of Jesus?' asked the one who was just like Hugh. With that, the other one reached into a big holdall and pulled out a small bible.

'No, no, not today, thanks,' said Nell, and she closed the door.

She sat on the floor inside the door and cried. This was supposed to be getting easier, she thought, as the tears flowed. You've always wanted to try writing. You promised yourself you would give it a real go and take your mind off the break-up. But oh no, what do you do? Sit around when you should be writing and disappear off into dreamland! You wouldn't take it from the kids at school! Get into that kitchen and make coffee and get down to some serious work!

Nell stirred her coffee, munched a chocolate biscuit and thought about her daydream. It would make a cat laugh, really, she thought. You off in Tuscany, on first-name terms with Muriel Spark, no less! And the subject of a scholarly biography! Patsy the watercolourist, that was the best yet! Sure Patsy couldn't draw a line! Still, though, she thought, I won't tell her about this daydream: it wouldn't do to be howling with laughter at the absurdity of the notion that Patsy was artistic! Interesting, too, isn't it, how the daydream focused on success with *Brown World* Oh yes, quite significant that it wasn't Sir Bashel O'Dell who was responsible for my biography being written!

*

Every old man I see
Reminds me of my father
When he had fallen in love with death
One time when sheaves were gathered

'Now, I am not going to give you any help here. Read the stanza yourselves quietly once or twice and get ready to answer my questions.' Nell perched her bottom on the radiator and looked around the room. 'Ready?' she asked. 'Caroline, who do you look like?'

'I don't understand, Miss Hynes.'

'When visitors come to your house and they see you, who do they say you look like? Your mother? Your father?'

'Me da, Miss Hynes.'

'Would it be a strange thing if someone said you looked like someone who wasn't related to you?'

'They might be tryin' to say your da or your ma were playin' away, Miss,' said Lisa.

'Indeed, that would be a normal reaction, but supposing they weren't trying to suggest that at all, would it be a strange thing to say?'

'It'd be bleedin' weird, Miss. You don't look like complete strangers,' said Martina.

'But look at the poem. What is the poet saying about his father?'

'All auld fellas look like him,' said Niamh.

'Good, Niamh. Now look carefully again at his words. Does he really say all old men look like his father, or does he say something more?'

'They all remind him of his da, Miss.'

'Well done. How do you think they might remind him of his father?'

'They way they walk and talk and the clothes they wear,' said Tracy.

'Good. Does that apply to old women too, do you think?'

'All my nana's friends get the same thing at the hairdressers, right? They all get a shampoo and set, and they wear the same clothes and they have false teeth and they go to bingo and Mass and they are real narky,' said Rachel.

'And Rachel, if your granny died and you were missing her and you saw one of those other old women, would they make you think of her?'

'Yeah.'

'Would that be painful, do you think?'

'If she was only just dead it might make you cry, but if she was dead ages it might be just nice to think of her.'

'Girls, do people want to die?'

'No.'

'But did the poet's father want to die?' Tracy folded her arms on the desk and rested her head on them. 'Miss Hynes,' she wailed, 'I don't get it. I hate poetry. I hate poems about death; we're always doing poems about death.

Can we not skip them?'

'No, we can't skip any poem because it could come up in the exam, and you are right that there are too many poems about death, but bad and all as it is for a seventeen-year-old, believe me it's ten times worse for an old woman like me. Now, nobody has told me yet why he says his father had fallen in love with death. Any ideas?'

'He wants to die, Miss.'

'Good, now why?'

'He's real old and sick.'

'Could be. Do you think he is lying in hospital in terrible pain or do you think he just dies peacefully at home after the harvest?'

'Peacefully, Miss Hynes,' said Rebecca.

'What is your reason for saying that, Rebecca?'

''Cos the harvest is done on the farm. He was there gathering the sheaves, and when they were gathered he died then.'

'Very good. Now I have very simple questions for homework . . . '

'Ah, Miss Hynes,' complained Niamh, 'we've done loads today, can we not talk?'

'No, Niamh. Now start writing, "Is stanza one sad? Give reasons for your answer, and . . . "'

'You're not giving us two questions, are you?' yelped Caroline.

'Two very short questions, yes. And the second one: "Is stanza one happy? Give reasons for your answer."'

'They're stupid questions, Miss,' growled Sharon. 'You expect us to say one thing one minute and then say the opposite.'

'Not really. Both sadness and happiness could be in the stanza.'

'Supposin' we can't see any happiness, does that mean we only have to answer one question?'

'No, Carol. You must write about why you think there is no happiness in the stanza.'

'But Miss Hynes, that's not fair,' said Debbie. 'We worked real hard today and then you give us two big mad questions for tomorrow.'

'Debbie, life's not fair. I am preparing you for life! Now there are four minutes left, are you going to begin the homework or talk quietly?'

'Talk, Miss,' they all said.

*

Nell ate her dinner quickly. She washed up and sat down to spend an hour or two at *Brown World* before she went to the writing class. It was vital to get some quality work done this evening: in a short while Sir Bashel O'Dell would get his most public airing to date. The chances were that her fellow students might approve of him; she needed to have some private quality work done to offset the shame she would feel.

She looked at what she had written on Sunday morning. Her character was in Harcourt Street. The street was white and spongy. Nell made a face at the written page. What utter rubbish! she thought. That is just like the advertisement on the television for chewy mints. How could that be a metaphor for anything? Her spirits sank, and she put down her pen. I'd be laughed out of it by any half-decent publisher. Imagine drawing on an advertisement for mints when trying to make a profound point about human existence; that won't do. She got up from the table and went to her room. She changed into her jeans and sweatshirt and went to the bathroom to brush her teeth. She scrubbed her gums vigorously and looked at her reflection in the mirror. 'You know, Nell Hynes,' she said to her reflection, 'for an intelligent woman, sometimes you can be very stupid.'

Picking up a manila folder and her jacket, she walked downstairs. She placed everything on the bottom step. Pop the Sir Bashel pages into the folder and I am ready for the off, she thought. All the time that remained before leaving was hers to work on *Brown World*. I'll have a cup of tea while I'm trying to work this one out, she decided, and she plugged in the kettle. On the other hand, she thought, as the kettle began to hum, think of all the advertising campaigns which are long since gone and forgotten – advertisements which had worked their way too into public awareness, unlike the one for chewy mints. Who today talks about Sally O'Brien 'and the way she might look at you' or 'His nibs, her nibs, in fact all nibs prefer Haughtons Superflow, true blue ink.' That was a cinema ad when Nell was a child; all the kids in her local cinema used to chant those words automatically when the little cartoon nibs appeared up on the big screen. If you said that today to someone, would it ring a bell? Probably not. And the sweet ad could be well finished by the time *Brown World* came out. I am not going to let that deter me, thought Nell. Anyhow, any good literary agent or editor will suggest the minor changes that might be needed. The kettle had boiled but she had no time for tea; she had some real writing to do before leaving for the class.

*I cut through an alley into Camden Street and looked up towards Rathmines. The clock tower was white, and so too were the mountains behind. I walked at a frantic pace, keeping my eyes firmly fixed on the pavement. Suddenly it seemed as though someone had upended a tin of paint across the flags of the footpath. Rivulets of colour flowed across the path and into the street. The colours which swirled about me were the normal colours; the path turned grey. I looked ahead – the sky was blue and Rathmines clock tower was red-brick once more. I did not feel pursued any longer, so I slackened my pace and headed for my apartment. Once there, I felt at ease. I sat on the sofa and thought about the day. Why had all this happened, I wondered? It was too much to be assailed by anguish, terror and dread twice in one day. Should I seek help? My options were limited: going to the GP was a non-starter – hysterical and hormonal, that was how he would describe me, the thirty-year-old brat, and then he would give me a fistful of valium. Help would have to come from a different quarter. I would talk to a friend, a friend who might know someone. But what real friend had I? Oh yes, I got by in this world of work and play, but whom did I really communicate with? Whom did I really trust?*

*I looked out the window of the apartment. Rathmines Road was crawling with people, scurrying along the footpaths in twosomes and threesomes, into shops, pubs and cafés. From my vantage point they all looked like ants, frantically moving towards worthless goals. What was the meaning of it all? Stupid even to utter that question; hadn't it kept Kant, Hegel, and Kierkegaard busy? How could I hope to shed some light on a question that had occupied minds of that calibre? I left the window and went to the desk. I picked up a notebook. I would keep a journal: that might help me to come to terms with whatever was going wrong, and if I found some professional who could help me through this terrible time, I would hand it to him or her when they asked me to describe how I was feeling.*

It was a quarter to seven, and Nell had to leave; there was not a lot of *Brown World* written. But she had overcome the initial hurdle and got something down on paper. She had more than adequately girded her loins against anybody at the writing class who might think the full extent of her talents lay with writing Sir Bashel O'Dell and all that old oirish paddywhackery. She closed the hall door and got into the car. A warm glow flowed through her as she drove to the grind-school complex. Nell Hynes was a force to be reckoned with. She was the business; she could create Sir Bashel, Lady Oonagh, Bridie and Cissy, make them speak credibly and at the same time create a minor public servant on the verge of breakdown in a deeply philosophical comment on life in *fin de siècle* Ireland.

# CHAPTER NINE

'A dull, grey, leaden, slate New York sky was above my cranium as I walked from the speakeasy. Of all the gin joints in all the world, why had the dumb floosie come to mine? I turned my collar to the cold and damp and walked into Lexington Avenue. Once my mob bosses knew Toots was back, they wouldn't trust me. I would wear a wire, snitch, sing to the cops, become a stool-pigeon, do anything for that woman's kisses. That dumb broad was my weakness, and Sam Giancana and the rest of them knew it. They would take me out to protect the operation. All I had built up from the rackets would be lost, and all because Toots wouldn't stay in Chicago like she promised she would.

'What the hell? I thought as I hung a left into Forty-third. Broads like her are a dime a dozen. She was about as rare as a grain of sand on the boardwalk in Atlantic City; come to think of it, that's where I met her. She was hustling, and I was just getting started for Sam in the numbers racket. Yeah, discussion is closed, I would take her out myself; no broad was going to mess up my future. I didn't care how hot the little mamma was! She was history. Sometimes a man's gotta do what a man's gotta do, as they used to say in the old neighbourhood all the time.

'I walked into Pacino's diner. Al was behind the counter. He slopped a grimy, wet dishcloth across the marble counter top. A dirty stub of black cigar hung from his nether lip.

"Joey," he called, "long time no see."

"Yup."

"Usual, Joey?"

"Yup."

"Gee! It's great to see ya, Joey. I hoird ya was doin' real good uptown."

"Yup." I had no time to make existential comment to Al. I had too much on my mind: I had to take Toots out before the mob took me out.

"Pastrami on rye, heavy on the mayo, ain't that right, Joey?"

"Yup."

"Never forget a customer, I never forget a customer. Coffee too, Joey?"

"Yup."

"Counter or booth, Joey?"

"Booth."

"Sure, Joey."

'I sat into the dark booth; the gloom therein suited my mood. Al knew well not to keep me talking. He hurried away and left me to my thoughts. Toots wouldn't be awake yet; she never woke before noon, and this morning she would be one tired girl; she and I had made love for hours. So long, Toots, I thought, and raised my coffee cup in a macabre toast to the only woman I had ever loved. In a couple of hours Toots would wake to spend her last day on earth . . . '

Tony Carmody finished reading and the class gave him a small round of applause.

'That's as far as I have got to date, Heather,' he said.

'It's about five hundred words. I know that's probably not a full chapter but it's as much as I could manage in a week.'

'And have you a sense of where the story is going?' asked Heather.

'I haven't got an outline committed to paper as such,' said Tony, 'but I have an idea of where my character is headed. These moments leading up to the murder of the gangster's moll are crucial. This is the greatest moral crisis he has ever faced. Now he has two choices: he can kill her and ensure his future as a big-noise gangster but move forever beyond redemption, or he can pull back and spare her life but face his own demise. Really, Heather, I'm not sure what he will do.'

'But that's really good. Your characters are taking on a life of their own, and that is the hallmark of all good writing. Tony, I jotted down some points as you were reading, things which need to be looked at whatever course the story takes. Will I read them now or will I wait until everyone has read?'

'Now, please, while the story is fresh in everyone's mind.'

'Fine,' said Heather. 'These points do not just apply to Tony's story; they apply to all creative writing. Feel free to jot them down yourselves. I also want you to give me your comments as well. First of all, Tony, well done; it's excellent. You have grasped that particular genre very well. The things which need tightening up are where you fail to maintain your credible links with your genre, where your language lets you down. For instance, your words like "therein", "existential" and "cranium". I feel they're too bookish to fit into the narrative. I would suggest you lose them and it would begin to work even better.'

'But Heather, isn't the hero meant to be, how will I put this . . . ? Say, for instance, if, as Tony says, he is facing a moral dilemma, how could his potential for redemption be suggested if he isn't distanced from the blood-and-guts narrative. Doesn't Tony need those words to suggest to us that he is different?' asked Una.

'No. I can see what you mean, but the trick is not to drop the heavy hint that this guy could change. What do you think, Tony?'

'I agree with Una. This guy isn't just a mindless thug, but the readers won't have any idea of that if I don't make some concessions to erudition; otherwise it's pure trash. I don't agree with you at all there; I would prefer to leave it.'

'As you wish,' said Heather. 'The other things which I am not too sure about are the references to Sam Giancana and placing him in the era of the speakeasy. Giancana belonged to the Kennedy years. if I am not mistaken, Bobby Kennedy, when he was the Attorney General, tried to clamp down on him . . .'

'Are you sure about that, Heather?' asked Tony. 'I think Giancana was the mobster who made a fortune during Prohibition and then got done on mail fraud.'

'That was Al Capone,' laughed Gerry.

'There's no need to laugh,' snapped Tony. 'Anyone can make an error.'

Brendan was sitting in front of Nell between Rose and Rita. Their three pairs of shoulders had been shaking with laughter as Tony read his story. Nell was getting nervous.

'So, Tony, ould son,' began Brendan, 'did you put in inverted commas, or what?'

'Where?' asked Tony, without looking around.

'For the "all the gin joints" and for "turned my collar

to the cold and damp"' Brendan only just made it to the end of his question. He concealed a snort of laughter with a big blow into his hanky.

'No, I did not.' replied Tony. 'There was no need. I wasn't lifting them, as you seem to suggest. Those words are my homage to Bogart and to Simon and Garfunkel; it's up to the readers to take them thus.'

'Thieving bloody magpie,' Rose whispered to Brendan and Rita.

'I am going to wrap up Tony's story,' said Heather. 'Tony, keep going – it shows great promise. I hope you feel all the criticism here is constructive. We have time for one more before the coffee break . . . '

'Heather?'

'Tony?'

'Before we move on, could you give me the names of some publishers?'

'At the end of the class I will put the name of a standard reference book on the board. This will be relevant to all here who wish to find out about publishing. Nell, you have been very quiet this evening. Could you read us yours please?'

Nell opened her folder. 'Heavens, you have been busy,' said Heather, as she spotted all Nell's Sir Bashel pages.

The whole class spun around and Nell was mortified. 'Ah, there's lots of other things here too,' she said, to take the harm out of it. 'There's pieces here going back years. I just shove it all in together so it won't get lost,' she added, to cover her confusion.

And so Nell Hynes went public with Sir Bashel O'Dell; her mother and Patsy didn't really count. She read the class the whole story even though that wasn't part of her plan. She was on a roll; they appeared to be enthralled, and she kept going. As she drew to a close she read more quickly, anxious to get it over and done with and concerned that the coffee break wouldn't be spoiled. The class broke into a round of thunderous applause and they all filed out into the little canteen. 'We will talk about Nell's story after coffee,' Heather Connolly called after them.

Nell sat at a table in the grind-school canteen. She stirred her coffee in great agitation. She tore the paper of the Twix bar and selected one finger; it was all happening just as she had predicted: they liked Sir Bashel O'Dell. She would make her mark on the world by writing a work of popular fiction! When it was published it would have a lurid cover; the title, whatever it might be, would be in embossed gold lettering; Isabella would be on the front; she would be very beautiful, wearing a long dress, and a hint of decollatage would be added for good measure. The novel would be swapped in offices, and women would snooze blissfully on the bus to Rathmines in the evenings having devoured a few pages. She bit into the chocolate, sipped her coffee and contemplated her future with dread.

After the break, Nell returned to her seat at the back of the room. Rose, Rita and Brendan slid in in front of her. 'Fantastic, Nell,' said Brendan with a big smile. 'I was just about to do the mob a favour and bash Tony's "cranium" until I heard yours!'

'Aren't you glad now you didn't?' joked Rose. 'Heather would have had to send for the guards; they would have come and carted you away, and you would have missed Sir Bashel!'

'Well,' said Heather to her class, 'what did you think of Sir Bashel?'

'Wonderful,' said Rose.

'Fabulous,' said Rita. 'I can't wait for next week. I'm

dying to find out what happens next.'

'I think it sould be made into a film,' said Clare over by the wall. 'I was thinking over the coffee who I would cast as Sir Bashel . . .'

'Funny, I was too,' said Brendan. 'It would have to be someone small, couldn't have a big healthy-lookin' fellow like Sean Connery. What about John Hurt? They could scrunch him up into a wheelchair easily, and he's gettin' on a bit, and he would look as if he had a past . . . '

'What about Daniel Day Lewis?' asked Rita. Brendan gave a big whoop of laughter. 'What's so funny about Daniel Day Lewis?' she asked him irritably. 'He is a great actor.'

'I know he is. It's just when you said his name I thought of all the articles I read about the kind of preparation he does for a role. You know, the way he stayed in character when he was playing Christy Brown, and he never left his wheelchair even for lunch. I just got the giggles wondering what he might do to prepare for the role of Sir Bashel O'Dell. Would he set himself a target of the number of women he would have before shooting began . . . for the sense memory, you know like.'

'Stop,' said Heather. 'Your enthusiasm is commendable, but I want you to discuss the writing; no more flights of fancy for the moment, keep them for the next chapter! I want to begin by saying to Nell that her story is superb, absolutely superb. This novel must be finished and must be submitted to a publisher,' beamed Heather.

Nell peeped through the blinds. Out on the street, buses were racing into town. She would like to be on the top deck of one of them, heading . . . anywhere!

'You must be delighted, Nell,' said Heather. 'It's a fantastic achievement. You have a real flair for writing;

keep it up.' Nell smiled weakly at Heather.

'Do you spend hours and hours at it?' asked Gerry.

What could she reply? The Sir Bashel story had poured forth from her with an ease and a speed which made her want to curl up and die! If she said she didn't spend much time on it and they thought it was wonderful wouldn't that seem like boasting? She would be like one of those people on cookery programmes who whipped out a perfect soufflé, smiled to camera and quipped, 'Here's one I made earlier.'

Imagine being seen to be proud of Sir Bashel! Worst of all, though, would be to say she had toiled and toiled over it all week. That would do nothing for her intellectual street cred. Thank God, at least that hadn't happened! But that Sir Bashel O'Dell was rapidly turning into an albatross round Nell's neck!

'I had the germ of an idea already,' lied Nell. 'That's why I was able to write a lot this week; it will probably be very different next time.'

'See,' said Heather. 'You were always a writer in the making.'

'Heather,' said Tony Carmody, 'could I come in here a moment?'

'Certainly.'

'What is troubling me about the accolades this story is getting here tonight is the fact that nobody has commented on its being mere pap – formulaic writing of mere pap. There's no intellectual bite to the thing at all, yet you have heaped praise on it. I thought the function of creative-writing classes was to enable us to produce something which follows in the noble literary tradition for which this country is famous. This is only women's fiction, bodice-ripper stuff . . . '

'Yes, Tony, I get your point,' said Heather, and she looked in consternation at Nell. 'I stand by my assertions that Nell's story is excellent, wonderfully written, within its genre, and no, I do not agree that the function of creative-writing classes is solely to produce work that will withstand the test of time. It would be wonderful if that happened, but the objective of this class is to get everyone expressing themselves first, and then, if possible, to get it published. Holding out for something supposedly better is just intellectual snobbery,' she finished.

'But my writing is terse; the style is lean; I have it honed to a minimum; my character is facing a moral dilemma . . . '

'Ah, give it a rest, Tony. You're only jealous,' snapped Gerry. 'The woman's story has all the essential ingredients of a good read, that's all Heather's saying. She didn't say it was *Anna Karenina.*'

'Jealousy has nothing to do with it, Gerry. This is an objective assessment of a piece of writing that is inherently flawed. The servants are one-dimensional stereotypes, all speaking in this stage-Irish language. She should be ashamed of herself . . . '

'We are going to have to stop there,' said Heather. 'You have made your views very clear, Tony. We will just have to agree to differ. I think it's wonderful. Now . . .'

Who does that fellow think he is? wondered Nell. Big ignorant lump, she thought, as she looked at the broad expanse of his back. Doesn't even have the manners to look at someone when he is addressing a remark to them. Sitting up there spilling out of his chair, all polyester and viscose and moral dilemmas. Holding forth about formulaic writing and mere pap. Sure that fellow couldn't stick to the bones of the simplest formulas. She wondered should she respond. The idea of defending Sir Bashel O'Dell was repugnant to her, but the fellow had some cheek. Just because Sir Bashel O'Dell wasn't Virginia Woolf didn't mean he was without merit: compared to Toots and Tony, Sir Bashel was a veritable jewel. Nell Hynes wasn't going to let any upstart tear poor Sir Bashel to pieces.

'Heather,' began Nell. She was very nervous; she hated conflict, but it had to be done. 'Before we move on, may I respond to some of what Tony said?'

'Certainly,' said Heather, though she looked a little pale.

'I am a little troubled by Tony's claim of objectivity,' Nell began. 'Perhaps we have slightly different views of the word. My story is without a doubt formulaic. I never claimed it to be anything more. But how someone can claim to have a lean and terse style and have a "dull", "grey", "leaden" and "slate" New York sky is beyond me! Tony's objective literary criticism seems only to extend to others' work – if it extended to his own surely he would have observed that verbose pretentiousness is a hallmark of his own endeavours and that the much-derided formulaic writing escapes him completely.'

Heather Connolly was going green at the gills. She pleaded with her eyes at Nell to stop; Nell pretended she didn't see her. Heather had been glad enough to let Nell fill an awkward space when Tony had been dominating the class, so she could suffer the consequences now.

'Formulaic writing shouldn't be held in contempt,' continued Nell. She was getting into her stride nicely now, as she addressed the stripes in Tony's Fair Isle sweater. 'Shakespeare's comedies and tragedies are formulaic. In Jane Austen the woman always gets her man. There's nothing wrong with formula, provided the writer has the talent to do something exciting and entertaining with it. But when the writer is manifestly unable to work to any formula and suffers from grandiose delusions . . . Gosh, Tony, I hope that's not a tautology. That would be very painful for a master of the laconic . . . '

'Nell, that's enough,' said Heather.

'You are quite right, Heather,' said Nell. 'It is enough, that is all I wanted to say.'

'Well,' continued Heather, with a quiver in her voice, 'feelings certainly did run high this evening, didn't they? That's good,' she added, without conviction. 'That shows how passionately you all feel about the work. I want you to continue with your novels for next week. We will be reading some more, but maybe just one or two. I want to begin discussing writing for radio. I have a handout prepared, so take one before you go.'

'Drink, Nell?' asked Rita and Rose.

'No, I'm expecting a phone call. See you next week; looking forward to hearing your novels.' She walked out of the classroom into the car-park and drove home.

When Nell opened her hall door she could hear the sound of her own voice on the answering machine's tape. It resounded spookily in the hall of her dark house. She switched on the lights and went to answer the phone. Barbara was beginning her message as she picked up the receiver.

'It's OK, I'm here, Barbara. I've just come in,' she said.

'Hi, Nell. How did it all go at the class? Nell, are you there?'

'Yeah, still here, just trying to get out of this sleeve,' she answered.

'Are you comfortable?'

'Fine now,' said Nell, as she slid the coat from under her.

'Did you read your story? Did they like it? Does what's-her-name think it could be published?'

'Barbara,' laughed Nell, 'that's three questions. I'll take them one by one: yes, yes and maybe.'

'Nell, stop messing. Give me a proper answer.'

'I did read my story, Barbara. The class liked it but I wouldn't mind them; we are all just learning. The teacher liked it too. She says I should keep going . . . '

'Oh Nell!' shrieked Barbara. 'That's fantastic. Now I was reading in tonight's paper that Maeve Binchy made millions last year. Just think, Nell! That could be you in a few short years. You could buy a house in Dalkey . . . '

'Barbara, stop. The teacher only said it was good. You're frightening me and you're losing the run of yourself. And anyway, my story is very lowbrow. I'm not sure if I want to be associated with something that's too popular. Everyone who has seen it so far thinks it's good, so it can't be art.'

'Art!' shouted Barbara. 'Who gives a twopenny damn about art? If you can write something that people will buy and enjoy, go for it. I wish I could write. And if I could, Nell, I am telling you I wouldn't be worrying whether it was art or not. I'd be lashing it down on the page and selling the movie rights. Don't think of giving up now.'

'I'm not giving up, Barbara. I will finish it, but I reserve the right to have artistic misgivings.'

'Yeah, yeah. Now tell me, any talent in the class?'

'She only had time to listen to two stories tonight and the fellow who read was . . . '

'Nell, I don't mean writing talent. Men, Nell, I mean

men talent. I know you hate me talking about Hugh, and I have respected that. But you were terribly cut up, and it's been months. Now might just be the time for a little recreational sex!'

'You are incorrigible, Barbara. I should have known you meant men,' laughed Nell. 'No, Barbara, nobody at all. In fact, they all look very married.'

'And why would you let a little thing like marriage put you off if the old chemistry was right?'

'I wouldn't, but there is no chemistry, or at least none that hit me instantly, and I haven't the interest or energy to forage. I am there to learn creative writing; it's not a spot of covert man-hunting.'

'Don't I know! Pure as the driven snow is our Nell,' teased Barbara. 'I was only thinking how nice it would be if, while developing your creative side, you also looked after your libido! Wouldn't it shorten the long winter evenings and take your mind off school?'

'I will keep an open mind, Barbara, I promise, but don't hold your breath,' and Nell shivered as she thought of Tony Carmody. 'It's nearly ten o'clock. I want to do a little bit of writing before I go to bed. I'm going to hang up now but I will ring you at the weekend.'

'Do that, and remember, Nell, I am thrilled for you. Don't turn your nose up at the talent you have because it's not the one you might have wished for. Keep writing. Night.'

'Night, Barbara, and thanks.'

Nell put down the phone. The house was cold and her coat lay beside her on the floor in a crumpled ball. She shook it out, hung it up and went to the kitchen. She put her writing folder on the counter and plugged in the kettle. She flicked through her Sir Bashel pages as she waited for the water to boil. If I keep going at this rate I'll have to buy another folder and another ream of paper, she thought. She poured her tea and went in to the living room. I am not writing tonight, she decided. I don't want to have too much done by next week. Staunch the creative flow now and again; that would be no harm – it would stop people thinking there was nothing at all to this writing business. She flopped onto the couch and consoled herself with the thought that, if Sir Bashel O'Dell were published to great popular acclaim, she could always use a nom de plume!

# CHAPTER TEN

'Nell, you're breaking up, I can hardly hear you,' said Mrs Hynes. 'Keep talking, though, and I'll try to make the best of it,' she continued. 'When are you coming home?' she asked, slowly enunciating her words, as though talking to a foreigner. But Mrs Hynes was on her own phone. Nell hadn't been having any difficulties hearing her; the problem was with this bloody useless mobile phone they had given her when she left Dublin. It was to have been her lifeline when she was far from friends and family, but so far it had been hopeless.

'It's going to be at least another three weeks,' said Nell. 'The weather has been very bad.'

'But didn't you need bad weather? The pages I read of your story all took place in bad weather. What's a novel set in Ireland without bad weather?'

'True, Mammy, but what we wanted was gloom, mists, a little bit of rain, atmospheric gloom – that kind of bad weather. What we have got is storms and torrential rain. Sir Bashel's castle blew down!'

'Good God!' said Mrs Hynes. 'Though right enough I did see something on *Nationwide* about bad floods and storms in the west. But I would never have thought Sir Bashel's castle would blow down.'

'Mammy, it wasn't a real castle. The OPW wouldn't let us use any of the real castles. A set designer made it and it was brought down from Dublin in sections, but it did hold everything up. The director is very cranky and we are all just sitting around waiting for the weather to improve. Tempers are getting very short. I would just love to get away for a day.'

'And why can't you?'

'Rewrites, Mammy, rewrites. The Lady Oonagh Glockamorrah never likes her lines.'

'The cheek of her objecting to your wonderful lines. When I think of the tripe that one has been in. Nell, do you remember her in . . . '

'Mammy,' warned Nell, 'you are not to mention her name or a single thing she has been in. You never know who might hear us.'

'All right so, but I still think she has a nerve. She ought to be down on her bended knees thanking you for the quality role you have put her way. Nell, can you not even get into Ballyvaughan and read the paper over a cup of coffee and get rid of them for an hour?'

'No, Mammy, I'm stuck here. It's like being on call, I suppose.'

'What's that, Nell? You're breaking up on me again.'

'Look, Mammy, you're losing a lot of this conversation. I'll hang up and try again some other time. Or maybe if I am lucky I will be able to slip into Ballyvaughan and ring from there. Take care. Bye.'

Nell put the phone on the kitchen counter of her mobile home. Of course the movie people didn't call it a mobile home; it was Miss Hynes's trailer. There were two other trailers beside hers which belonged to the screenplay writers. These screenplay writers were in truth much busier than Nell. They dealt with all the rewrites; she was merely on hand to be consulted as a matter of courtesy. Once the movie rights of Sir Bashel had gone to auction he was no longer Nell Hynes's property. They had taken her novel and transposed it to a different medium. Nell had quaked at some of what had been done to poor little Sir Bashel, but she had no real powers of veto. In a sense she didn't care: she was laughing all the way to the bank. In one fell swoop the movie deal had given her more money than she had earned in twenty years teaching. Furthermore, for each day she spent in the trailer consulting the screenplay pair she was paid a retainer. And each of the retainers was more than a teacher's monthly salary!

But Nell Hynes hadn't completely prostituted herself. Beside the phone on the counter top lay her *Brown World* notebook. Moreover, it was nearly full, and a fresh one lay underneath it at the ready. While the two screenplay writers next door mangled poor old Sir Bashel O'Dell beyond Nell's recognition, she had been beavering away at *Brown World*. She would soon have enough pages to send off to a publisher. She sat on the couch. Publishers for *Brown World* could be tricky. There would be no question of sending it to the house which had taken Sir Bashel O'Dell; it just wasn't their sort of thing. They also wouldn't be too pleased if she were to be seen to be devoting her creative energies to another project when really she ought to be concentrating on the Sir Bashel sequels. That was what she had agreed with them when they signed the three-book deal. She would have to go and seek out some different houses herself – snooty outfits who wouldn't throw her a second glance if they heard she was even remotely connected with something as lowbrow as Sir Bashel.

She leaned from the couch to the coffee table and wondered what she might sample as she thought about publishers. The coffee table groaned under an array of food and drinks. Every morning a delivery boy knocked on her trailer door with a food hamper: cheeses, breads olives and handmade chocolates. All these plus a never-ending supply of teas and coffees. But she confined herself to a mug of hot coffee and one black olive. She chewed the olive and sipped her coffee; then she smiled. What are you worrying for? she asked herself. When you get back to Dublin, send the pages off to some crowd who don't deal in popular fiction; they'll be so grand they'll never have heard of you!

Nell stood up and stretched her limbs. She looked out the window of her trailer. Smoky rain flew across the landscape and a sharp wind was still blowing. She craned her neck to the left but she still couldn't see the Aran Islands. To her right Ballyvaughan and Black Head were shrouded in grey mist. But the floods had subsided, the roads were opened again and work on the film had resumed. Nell picked up her rain gear and decided to go for a walk. Trailer fever would really kick in if she spent much longer alone.

A gust of wind slapped the door of the trailer back against its sides, but she closed it and began to walk up the slippy path of the sand dunes at Fanore Strand. She wouldn't take the path to the beach for her walk: it would be too exposed. If she continued up to the main road it wouldn't be so mucky and she would also see some faces who might just be willing to chat between scenes. She passed the screenplay writers' trailer; she could hear their voices coming in low, urgent whispers. They were both sitting at a desk in the window. Sophie waved weakly at Nell, but Naomi threw open the window.

'Well for some,' she sang out in her piping English accent. 'What I wouldn't give for a nice stroll in the Burren instead of being cooped up here in this roasting trailer and all because bleedin' madam Lady Oonagh Glockamorrah . . .' The wind whistled through the rest of her words.

Nell paused under their window. 'Still giving you grief, is she?' she asked.

'Major, major grief,' said Sophie through clenched teeth. 'Look at what she has put us through since break-fast,' added Naomi, as she pointed to two full ashtrays and a row of used coffee mugs.

'Girls,' said Nell, 'that trailer is a health hazard. Come out with me for a short walk. Give one of the little valeting lads a call. Get him to fumigate the place while you are out and return to it refreshed. Sophie looked tempted, but Naomi interjected, 'We can't, Nell; it's a nice idea but we have to get her sorted by lunchtime.'

'What's wrong with her now?' asked Nell.

'She has refused to do a bedroom scene with the bard, says the chemistry isn't right,' explained Naomi.

The bard?' shrieked Nell. 'I don't remember anything about any bard.'

'Don't worry about it, love,' said Sophie quickly. 'Alless-andro just wanted a love interest for the Lady Oonagh. He told us to write in a bard, so we did. Sasha was cast as the bard . . . '

'But aren't Sasha and and and . . . what's-her-face – That one who is playing the Lady Oonagh – aren't they an item? I am sure I read that in some magazine. How could there be a problem with chemistry?' spluttered Nell. 'We will never get home at this rate.'

'But Nell,' giggled Sophie, 'you're not up to date. They aren't an item any longer. Haven't you noticed a certain trailer rocking ever so suspiciously in the dead of night, rocking too much even for these awful storms?' As she paused for breath she nodded fiercely in the direction of a trailer farther up the path. Nell followed the direction of Sophie's nods: there, almost hidden in a cluster of sand dunes, was the most luxurious trailer on the location. It belonged to Sir Bashel O'Dell!

Nell turned back to Sophie and Naomi. 'But what's she on about, "The chemistry isn't right"?' said Nell to the two, who were now hanging out their trailer window. 'If she and Sir Bashel are an item, won't there now be chemistry where there shouldn't be any?'

'Yes,' said Naomi. 'But there are no on-screen intimacies between those two, not even a flashback to when they were coupling to produce little Bashel, Cashel and Dashel. Just supposing when they were doing a scene there was a tiny frisson between them, and say that Bashel bloke got a little hot and bothered, all they would have to do was tuck him into his bath chair a little more tightly.'

'Do you think you'll be able to find a way out of these difficulties?' asked Nell.

'Well,' said Sophie, 'now, Nell, you're not to let on we told you this, but just as you walked under the window we had cracked it, or rather we came up with something which might just work.'

'But we're not exactly going to rush up to the location with our rewrites just yet! Not after all the hassle she has given us,' added Naomi with a naughty grin. 'Let the bitch suffer. She's up there in her nightie under a big umbrella. We told her that if she refused to do the bed scene there would be a price to pay.'

'Like what?' queried Nell.

'Well, we told her we would have no choice but to sublimate the Lady Oonagh's sexual but unconsummated desire for the bard . . . '

'And?' said Nell.

'Look, Nell, come in can't you? I don't want them to hear us. You know how voices carry in the countryside.'

'Into that smelly little trailer? No way.'

'Ah please! The window was open all the time we were talking to you. Anyway, it's part of your contract to be on hand for essential script consultations!'

'Yes,' laughed Nell, 'but not to be aiding and abetting the settling of scores,' and she climbed the steps to their trailer and plonked herself on the couch.

'So how are you proposing to sublimate the Lady Oonagh's desires for the bard?' she asked wearily. All she wanted to do was go for a walk and get some air. So far she had travelled a mere six feet from her own trailer.

Sophie and Naomi picked up a large sheaf of pages fresh from the printer and shoved them over to Nell.

'Do I have to?' she pleaded.

'Yes,' they chimed in unison. 'Don't be put off by the number of pages − some are blank; we just want to show that patronising, temperamental cow that we are not to be trifled with. And we will talk you through it. You don't have to read every last word,' said Naomi.

'Right,' began Sophie. 'Lady Oonagh, attractive woman, has needs, can't be met by Sir B, wouldn't want them to be anyway when she finds out what the randy little so-and-so's been up to before he met her. Now in your novel, Nell, you didn't deal with this. That was fine in the novel. But, Nell my dear, we need bums on seats in the Omniplexes, we need . . . '

'Sex, and lots of it,' said Naomi. 'Hence the bard, which was fine and dandy when the two of them were at it regular on and off screen . . . '

'But we're buggered now that they're not,' continued

Sophie. 'So sublimated sexual desire might do the trick. I told her I was a Ken Russell fan, and as I said it I looked meaningfully at that dolmen . . . '

'She is terrified she is going to be stretched naked on that dolmeny thing and be forced to rub Burren plants all over her erogenous zones,' laughed Naomi, 'or that we have a spot of self-mutilation lined up for her.'

Sophie was squealing with delight at this. 'I really liked that one. Think, Nell, of how long she would have to be in make-up! She would have to leave the heaving and rocking trailer very early to be mutilated!'

'Can't see any lying on dolmens or self-mutilation here,' said Nell as she skimmed through the sheets. 'All I can see is a lot of slow caressing of props . . . '

'Yes, but they're all phallic-shaped objects belonging to the bard, Nell. She will linger over those caresses; music will play. She will fondle her neck with his quill, stroke his musket . . . '

'And outside in the spilling rain yer man the bard is runnin' around with hardly a stitch on him callin' her name.' Nell summed up what she saw on the remaining sheets.

'Exactly,' they said.

'Girls,' said Nell, 'isn't this terrible tripe?'

'Cheer up, Nell,' Sophie advised. 'It's not too bad. When we were working on arthouse stuff, we were starving. Think of the money and enjoy your walk.'

Nell left their trailer and took the narrow path to the main road. The road was closed to all traffic for the duration of the filming. Its tarmacadam dressing had been removed for a stretch of a few miles, and rough grass had been sown again in the centre; in a trice all traces of a secondary road had been removed and a narrow cart track had taken its place. There was a wide verge at the other side of the main road; in summertime it was used as a picnic area. But during the filming it was the parking bay for the catering, make-up and hairdressers' trailers. Sir Bashel's carriage was parked there too when it wasn't needed for shooting. All the shooting was taking place deep in among the crags of the Burren. A JCB had cleared some of the rocks and a crane had winched in Sir Bashel's castle panel by panel. The flat area which had been cleared was used to form a yard around the castle; outhouses and stables had been built too. That area was strictly no admittance except on business. Nell had been allowed through and had gone several times out of curiosity. But her initial curiosity had waned; most of the proceedings were a complete mystery to her: lots and lots of jargon, yards and yards of cable, wires and big fluffy microphones held over actors' heads.

The rain stopped; a watery winter sun tried to poke through the clouds. Nell pulled down the hood of her jacket. It was still very cold; a sharp wind blew, zinging along the telegraph wires. It squashed Nell's clothes into the contours of her body and plastered her hair back into her head. She put her hands into her pockets and stood and looked around her. She looked out towards Galway Bay; the sea was green, purple and grey like a day-old bruise; white horses edged the angry, choppy waves. But in summer, on a good day, the sea was navy and the grey Burren rocks soaked up the day's heat and were warm to the touch until late in the evening.

Nell realised with a start that her arm felt sore and she heard a voice calling.

*

'Nell,' said the voice urgently. 'Nell, for goodness sake, you can't daydream now.' Nell shook herself. She felt a tickling feeling about her knees; she heard the whispers of falling sheets of paper. She looked around; she was sitting in a plastic chair in a large room, and all her colleagues were there too. Olivia was beside her and the whisperings she heard were her In Service Day handouts slipping to the floor as she relaxed more fully into her reverie. Nell picked up the handouts and looked around her; the clock on the wall said ten thirty: another half an hour before coffee break.

She felt her arm sore again. It was Olivia digging her in the arm. 'Where were you?' she mouthed

'Clare,' answered Nell. Olivia arched her eyebrows and smiled at her; she turned her wrist to Nell, pointing the face of her watch towards her; she tapped at the little eleven on her watch face with her painted fingernail. Nell nodded. Yes, she would fill her in on everything at break.

The speaker at the top of the room placed an acetate sheet on to the overhead projector; there was just one word on his sheet and he covered it. 'We're going to do a little brainstorming session first,' he smiled. 'In considering the role of the teacher in the new millenium we need to look at where we see ourselves. Is our role crucial? Are we redundant? Are we a powerful group or is the teacher in present-day society disempowered? He passed blank pages to all his listeners. They were to make a list of all the words which best described their role. A buzz of talk filled the room. Nell looked to Olivia, who was scribbling furiously. 'How are you defining yourself as you face the new millennium?' she asked.

'Nell, I'm only colouring. I can't think of anything.' Olivia was drawing little matchstick men; she was giving

137

some glasses and some moustaches.

'One more minute,' called the speaker.

'Quick, Nell, think of something.'

'Truth or jargon?' asked Nell.

'Bit of both I suppose; let's cover all our options,' said Olivia, matter-of-factly.

'Pastoral care?' questioned Nell. 'Or is that a little too twee?'

'No, no, we nurture all the time,' said Olivia, and she wrote it down. So did Nell, but she put it further down her list so it didn't look as if they had copied each other.

'Right,' said the speaker, 'let's resume.' Nell scribbled quickly and added 'nag', 'nark', 'points getter' and 'something holy to do with God and religious things'.

'What did you write all those for?' hissed Olivia.

'Olivia Colleran, have you no sense? I wrote them because that's the kind of nonsense I'm supposed to write.' Nell turned to Olivia, looked her straight in the eye and began: 'Whilst I see myself primarily in a pastoral role, society today forces our young people to define their own sense of intrinsic self-worth by how many points they achieve in the Leaving Cert. Therefore, the pastoral facet of my calling has to be subordinated to the dictates of the exam system. Many students too see the only careers worth pursuing as those which demand really high points; they cannot be blamed for this since society has very rigid ideas as to which professions have status. Students overreach themselves in order to get into these professions, and the teacher who counsels otherwise is just a nag or a nark,' said Nell, without pausing for breath. 'Oh, and I included the holy something to do with God business 'cos I'm also doing all this while promoting the Christian ethos. Sure 'tis no wonder I have no time to teach!'

'Do you know what?' laughed Olivia.

'What?'

'You're the deviousest, cynicalest, slyest wagon that I ever came across.'

'I could say all that very slowly and sincerely too, though, Olivia, should the need arise,' said Nell.

They turned to face the speaker again. 'What I want to do now,' he began, 'is to evaluate what you have come up with, to compare it with what the latest educational research shows the role of the teacher to be, to measure as it were, what they say in the think-tanks and policy development units with what is being said by those at the chalk face, because in the final analysis it's those at the chalk face who really matter,' he smiled.

'And if it's very different, does that mean that the research is a load of nonsense or that we are all off our heads?' asked Ted Falvey, with a wide grin.

'Neither,' said the speaker very carefully. 'We coexist, pool and share all our ideas; it's a cross-pollination, as it were.'

'Ouch,' said Nell. Someone had prodded her shoulder blade sharply. She turned around.

'Bollocks, isn't it, Nell?' said Joe Grealish.

'Now I need a different kind of participation from you,' said the speaker. 'I want you to look at the overhead. See the word I have covered? Now I am going to reveal just one letter. I want you to guess what the word is. And before we begin, let me say that in a recent pilot study conducted in Nebraska, 94 per cent of teachers used this word as a key word to define their role.' The speaker rocked back and forth on his toes as he spoke. He pulled the sheet a little to one side and uncovered the letter 'h'.

'God, ye have me there,' laughed Gerry Vaughan.

'Hostile?' suggested Ted Falvey.

'Gimme a break,' hissed Olivia. Nell leaned back in her chair; she wasn't even going to try to play this silly guessing game. In the distance she thought she could hear music. The speaker pulled the little sheet over and he revealed an 'o'. Nell strained to hear the music better; she could hear singing too. And then she remembered: the sixth years were on retreat today. They were down in the hall practising for the Mass.

The speaker must have grown tired because this time he revealed the rest of the word in one go; maybe he had sneaked a look at his watch and seen that it was almost time for coffee break. The word was holistic; 90 whatever per cent of teachers in Nebraska saw their role as being holistic. Nobody in the room had chosen that word. The speaker went to his flip chart; he drew a big circle and added a second circle, allowing part of it to overlap into the first one. Into the circle on the right he wrote the word 'holistic', and into the circle on the left he wrote a random selection of words which he had found most frequently in the audience.

'Oh, spare me! sighed Ted Falvey.

Nell drifted back to Clare until the speaker decided it was time to release them for a break.

'Well you've all done great work this morning,' he said. 'Let's reconvene again in half an hour.'

'Tea or coffee, Olivia?' asked Nell, as Olivia headed for the toilets.

'Tea please, Nell, and Nell, find a seat well away from Marshall McLuhan.'

Nell laughed and walked towards the staffroom. Tracy and Niamh were standing outside the staffroom door.

'Hi, Miss Hynes,' said Tracy, 'jeh miss us?'

'No, although, come to think of it . . . forget it, no, I

do not miss the two of you.'

'Ah, Miss Hynes,' they whimpered, 'yer so crooool.'

'True, but then, girls, I am not on retreat. I am not overflowing with Christian kindness and charity.' Nell turned to go into the staffroom.

'Oh, Miss Hynes, please don't go in yet; we've some-thin' to ask yeh.'

'Be quick about it; we have to get back to the seminar, and I'd like a cup of tea first.'

'You ask her,' urged Niamh.

'I'm not bleedin' askin' her. You promised if someone narky came along that you'd do the askin',' said Tracy. 'Ah, Miss Hynes, I'm sorry, I didn't really mean that,' she said.

'Spit it out or I'm going,' said Nell.

'Miss Hynes, the fellow that's givin' the retreat is in there havin' his tea.' said Niamh, 'We can see him every time the door opens . . . '

'And he is drop-dead gorgeous, Miss Hynes, honest . . . '

'Oh, Miss Hynes,' swooned Niamh, 'he is a ride . . . ' Tracy gave Niamh a thump. 'You can't say things like that to Miss Hynes,' she said.

'Girls, where's all this leading?' She looked at her watch.

'Miss Hynes, we have very private notes to give him. Will you pass them on to him inside please? Please!' asked Niamh

'Certainly not. God knows what filth is in them!' Nell went in the door.

'Miss Hynes, we're dying,' they called after her, and they twisted their necks to catch a look at their idol.

'Not at all, girls, you'll be fine tomorrow,' smiled Nell.

# CHAPTER ELEVEN

Nell sniffed the air appreciatively: she breathed in the lavender oil which was burning in a pottery burner in the essential-oils section of the health-food shop. Old-fashioned canvas sacks of pulses and grains were stacked on the shop's bare scrubbed floorboards. Misshapen loaves and wholesome snacks were displayed in baskets on the counter. This evening Nell was free to browse: thanks to the seminar she had taught no classes, picked up no copybooks.

She left the school at four o'clock and drove to Rathmines. She had no pressing messages. She could wander, as the spirit moved her, from shop to shop. She might even stop for a coffee to let the evening's traffic pass before she headed for home and an evening's writing. Many of Nell's students worked in shops. They shuffled lethargically along the corridors at school and yawned their way through her classes. But once the last bell rang they metamorphosed into creatures of extraordinary energy. They dashed home, dumped their school bags, changed into stripey tracksuit bottoms, had a complete make-over and were there at their tills to take a pound coin from Nell as she paid for the paper. Nell often marvelled at how they did it, but she never asked.

These girls never worked in health-food shops; they stood behind the counters of newsagents – deep counters which sloped down to the customers and where the newest recruit filled up the space with Wispas, Wispa Mints and Wispa Golds. The staff in newsagents' shops didn't like customers: they preferred to chat. Nell knew that the only way to get attended to was to stand midway between two who were chatting, hold up what she intended to buy and hand the nearest one the money. It was different in health-food shops; the staff were older and the women didn't wear any make-up. Scrubbed as their shops' bare floor-boards, they were, and it didn't matter which of the city's many health-food shops Nell frequented, everyone working there had the same smell. Nell loved that smell. It didn't come from any conventional range of body sprays and deodorants that Nell knew intimately from the young girls at school. It was a fusion of smells from all the shops' products: the grains, pulses, fresh breads, oils and soaps. It exuded from every stitch of their woolly jumpers and from every swirl of their long cotton skirts as they walked.

Nell fingered some notebooks. They were German imports; wire-bound and made from recycled paper. Each grey page had a woodland scene in the top right-hand corner. There wasn't really much room for writing on any of the pages but Nell liked them. She picked one up. It would do to keep in her pocket as she went about her business. Nell was addicted to notebooks and scribbling in them in coffee shops. She smiled, fantasising that someday pages from one of these notebooks might be sold off for a hefty sum at Christie's or Sotheby's – if she ever made her name as an author, that was.

A tiny girl sat on the floor just where Nell was choosing the notebook. She was wearing a smock from a very expensive Montessori school. As she sat there she played with her teddy, discussing aloud what she would prepare for his dinner and holding imaginary consultations with him in a lovely little lisping voice. She held up packets of noodles and wholewheat pasta for his approval. But Teddy was having none of them. She moved on to the pear and apricot spreads and the cranberry juice and Nell stepped around her and went to pay for the notebook. The child's mother was at the desk.

'Try her on soya milk, a completely dairy-free diet,' the man behind the counter was saying to the woman. 'You'll see, it will do wonders for her asthma.' The man behind the counter was tall; his eyes were vividly blue and his hair was iron-grey. He smiled at the woman as he spoke. It was nearly November but he was still wearing Birkenstock sandals; long, long bare toes poked out through the leather thongs.

The woman went to the fridge and took some soya milk. 'Absolutely dairy-free?' she queried.

The man wasn't ready to serve Nell so she busied herself reading the shop's noticeboard. Wholefood cooking courses, macrobotic cookery demonstrations and healing weekends were all on offer. Most of them seemed to be taking place in Wicklow and most, to judge by the names of the people listed as contacts, were German. A whole different lifestyle was advertised here; if she were searching for one, Nell would have been hard pressed to decide which to choose.

'Absolutely dairy-free seems a bit dreary for a little girl, don't you think?' asked the woman. 'How shall I explain to her that ice creams and chocolate bars are banned for ever? Not,' she added hastily, 'that she ever ate much gunge, but this,' and she looked in dismay at her basket and then over to her daughter, still coaxing Teddy to decide on his tea, 'this seems very austere.'

'We have some treats in the freezer cabinet,' said the

man, 'soya yoghurts and soya ice creams too.'

The woman went to the freezer cabinet again. Nell continued reading. An astrologer's name was listed and it was a Rathmines number. Nell wondered should she get her chart done. Nell made a note of it: she might just go for it if it wasn't too expensive. Who knew how the planets were placed when Nell Hynes was born? Nell for sure didn't. Maybe having a real chart done by a proper astrologist might explain this sudden middle-aged burst of creativity she was experiencing. The woman was stacking up her dairy-free goods. The man still wasn't ready to serve Nell. He didn't mind how long his customers took and the woman wasn't rushing. Nell inhaled more lavender; she didn't mind either. She listened to the tape of some Eastern-sounding music playing very low in the background. Their calm brimmed over on to Nell. Just being in this shop made her feel well. If she shopped here, ate their food, took evening primrose oil, burned lavender oil, she could face anything. The yoga books on the shelves showed her it was possible to be lithe and supple into her seventies and the menopause books would see her through all that without ever having recourse to a HRT patch.

'Carob,' said the man. The woman had a large pile of goods on the counter by now and Nell's stomach was beginning to rumble.

'Mmmm?' said the woman, rooting for her credit card.

'Carob,' he said again. 'Anytime you feel like giving her a little chocolatey treat, give her some carob instead; tastes just as nice but without anything harmful.' The woman added a few packets of carob drops to her pile and the man started to add it all up. '£34.72 please,' he said, and Nell moved nearer to the till. The woman took no plastic bags. She arranged all her groceries in a big wicker basket and left the shop with her little girl.

'Be sure to let us know how she is doing,' he called after her.

Nell paid for her notebook and went out into the mall. It was cold out there; the tiles were wet and smeared with leaves and muddy footprints. At the end of the mall through the doors to the street Nell could see the evening traffic slowing to a snail's pace along the Rathmines Road. She zipped her winter jacket and walked into the coffee shop. The jumbo breakfast was still on the menu as Nell peeped in over the counter to get a closer look at the food. Nell's stomach heaved as the girl behind the counter sloshed beans over rashers, eggs, hash browns and sausages. The girl plopped a fried egg on top of the beans and handed the brimming plate to a big fellow in plaster-stained overalls. Nell took a tongs and selected a Danish pastry, poured a coffee and went to pay.

All the reserves of serenity and well-being she had built up from her browse in the health-food shop were in danger in the shopping centre's coffee shop. Family parties could wipe her calm out in seconds; one 'wah' from a sticky baby in a high chair could unravel it completely. Nell stood in the middle of the coffee shop looking for the ideal spot. She wanted a large table where she could spread out, and an upholstered seat, not a hard chair. Spotting just the one she wanted in a far corner she went to sit down. Nell sighed contentedly as she slid her bottom in along the soft seat and put her tray on the table. She opened her jacket and let it slide down around her hips, not bothering to fold it. She would be sorry when she went to put it on again; it would be creased. But she was tired and hungry and she didn't really care.

An itch overwhelmed her: an itch which would only be satisfied when she began to scribble in her new notebook. She sliced the Danish, took a mouthful of coffee and reached down into her coat pocket for the notebook. Small germs of ideas swirled about in her brain; she licked the icing from her fingers and opened the notebook. 'Health Food Shop,' she wrote. 'And my musings therein,' she continued. Pretentious twaddle, she scolded herself, and promptly drew a big line through that. But she did want to capture her feelings on paper about the shop – about all the different shops in shopping centres, in fact. Somewhere deep inside her she knew that the bones of a profound thought were hidden in what she felt about shopping centres! And if she could just begin to articulate on a page, she could tease it out into something that she could develop for *Brown World*. She took a bite of Danish and another sip of coffee. 'Health-food shops versus newsagents,' Nell scribbled this time. She put down her pen and rested her chin on her hands. Why, she wondered, as she looked around the coffee shop, do I feel so wonderful in one shop and so wretched in another? She thought about newsagents' shops and all that she hated about them. She pictured the shelves of magazines, piles of newspapers on the floor, yards and yards of counter space taken up by chocolate bars, and the rotating stands of birthday cards and fat paperbacks. People spewed forth from buses each evening and went straight into a news-agent's, cars half-mounted the kerbs, and their drivers flicked on the hazard lights while they popped in for a packet of Featherlite Durex and a few wobbly carnations.

'Seats of urban malaise,' wrote Nell, 'as opposed to oases for the mind, body and spirit.' That was more pretentious twaddle but she could untwaddle it later into a few *mots justes* for *Brown World*. A brown skin was forming on her coffee and the Danish was finished. Nell closed her notebook. A girl was stacking the chairs on to the table beside Nell, and her colleague was washing the floor. Nell got up, put on her coat and side-stepped past the yellow plastic 'cleaning in progress' sign. She hurried out of the shoping centre and headed for home, determined to get some real writing done.

\*

*Isabella sat at the small table in her room at Burren Castle. Some blank pages lay before her; writing to her mother was proving very difficult. Convincing her mother that she might be in danger from the dastardly Sir Bashel O'Dell was impossible. She had no virtue left to speak of since Barney, so why should her mother worry if she were in danger from the crazed advances of her depraved employer? Perhaps her mother knew the full story about Sir Bashel all along and intended to punish her by casting her adrift in this wild and rude land amidst these coarse people. She looked at her page: 'Dearest Mamma,' was all she had written. A tear fell; it smudged the ink; some more tears fell. Isabella put down her pen and collapsed on the little table in a terrible fit of weeping. Could her mother be capable of such duplicity? Was she really cut off forever from her family and friends with no one at all to care whether she perished or not? And then she heard that strange sound again, a scratching sound as though a mouse were nibbling at the wainscoting. She lifted her head from the table top and blew her nose: she was determined to discover what was making the sound; she could never collect her thoughts for the letter to her mother if she had to listen to that infernal scratching. Standing up, Isabella began to pace her room; the* sound wasn't coming from within at all. She drew back her curtains and threw open her large casement; she recoiled in terror as she heard a man scream; the scream was stifled quickly but it was followed by the most dreadful oaths. In the darkness she could see that a great clump of the ivy which covered the walls of Sir Bashel's castle had been wrenched from the wall. The ivy swung to and fro in the night air. Whatever can have happened? she wondered. It wasn't an especially windy night. She pulled the casement closed but as she did so she heard that horrible man's voice again. This time he spoke in a loud and urgent whisper.

'For the love and honour of God, woman, is it tryin' to kill me entirely yeh are?' the voice hissed at her in the darkness but still Isabella could not see from whom it came. Fear gripped her; terror mounted in her bosom. What mad Irishman was out there? Was he trying to get at her? Or was he merely a spirit called forth to torment her in her exile in this wild country? She looked out the casement again and saw the piece of ivy jutting from the castle wall, and this time she noticed a figure clinging to it for dear life.

'Help, for God's sake, can't yeh? This thing is goin' to give way any minute.'

'Who are you?' Isabella called into the darkness.

'Stop askin' silly questions and gimme down yer hand before I break me neck.'

'Whoever you are,' she said primly, 'you are very much mistaken if you think I am going to thrust my hand out blindly into the darkness and aid a perfect stranger into my room. You might be a scoundrel or a reprobate.'

The ivy creaked in the gentle night breeze; whoever was out there was in real danger; something softened within her.

'Miss Isabella,' he said. 'Yer in no danger at all. 'Tis only me, Tadhg O'Flanagain, file – the bard to you. Gimme yer

149

*hand and let me in, please Miss Isabella. I'm cut to ribbons on this oul' ivy.' Isabella's eyes had grown accustomed to the gloom of the Burren night and she saw now that it was indeed Tadhg, Sir Bashel's bard. She stretched out her hand and helped to pull him up to her window ledge. When he was out of danger he sat up on the ledge to draw his breath. Isabella shivered at the sight before her. He had a long mane of filthy, red hair and a luxuriant beard. His face was covered in blood and his kilt was torn; huge, dirty, muscular thighs were to be seen beneath the jagged tears in his kilt . . .'*

That's ticking over nicely, thought Nell, as she sat writing her Sir Bashel story at the kitchen table. God, I'd be finished in jig time if I had a few more nights like this with no corrections. She put down her pen and went to pour herself some tea. Not happy with the bard wearing a kilt though; that'll have to go; it's not authentic. Bit too Hollywoody for my tastes! Time enough to dress him in a kilt when and if the movie rights are sold; the director can put what he likes on him then and I won't care a hang! Nell's giggles filled the quiet of the kitchen. Movie rights indeed, she giggled, recalling her daydream. Get a grip on yourself, woman! Her tea slopped along the table as she laughed; she pulled her Sir Bashel notebook out of the way of the dribbles. 'And where, Miss Hynes,' said Nell, as she wiped the table with a J-cloth, 'where did you get the idea for the character of the bard?' 'A daydream,' said Nell, in a very grand and solemn tone. 'He came to me in a daydream; some of my finest creations have their origins in daydreams . . .'

Nell stopped giggling, squeezed out her cloth and took up her position again at the table. You, she admonished herself, are worse than Tracy and Niamh any day. You wouldn't tolerate any giggling in class from them when there's work to be done. Sit down there, start writing, take the kilt off that fellow, put a pair of trousers on him and get on with the story! Don't you know that if it's funny it can't be good? Nell picked up her pen and bit it. But can he still be a sexy dog like he was in my little reverie? Of course he can, she thought. Why spurn a perfectly legitimate source of inspiration? Once more she began to scribble.

*'The blessin's a God on yeh, Miss Isabella, yeh saved me life.' The bard placed a big dirty paw on Isabella's shoulder and he levered himself from the casement ledge into her bedroom. 'And me reputation,' he added, giving her a lascivious grin. He landed with a great thud on her floor. Isabella felt herself starting to retch.*

*'Take your filthy hands off me immediately,' she said, 'or I shall scream for Thady and he will have you seen off the premises this instant.' The bard flopped onto Isabella's bed, pulled off his boots and stretched out on the counterpane.*

*'Well, yeh impudent little English minx yeh! Yeh don't mean to tell me that yeh thought it was yerself I was after, do yeh?'*

*'Well, you were climbing up to my room. What was I supposed to think? And in this strange country I never know what to expect.'*

*'For the love an' honour a God, girl; what'd make me think of yeh! With yer pale English complexion and yer mincin' ways. Haven't I the finest a Irishwomen only dyin' for me? Haven't yeh read any a me poems? I broke hearts all over Clare and Galway, deed 'n I did! And as far off as Roscommon too.' With that the bard broke into a most fearsome caterwauling, in Gaelic – for Isabella understood not a syllable.*

*'Quiet,' she said, 'do you want to disturb the entire castle?*

Have you no concern for my reputation? What is to become of me if you are discovered in my room? What would the Lady Oonagh Glockamorrah say if she were to learn that you were in my chamber? My life would be intolerable! Think of the sniggering in the servants' quarters!'

'Tell me, Miss Isabella, are all the English as stupid as yerself? How long is it now that yer here? Six months? Sure it must be that at least. And not a word of the Irish are yeh after learnin'. That song I sang is a love song. And 'tisn't dedicated to you. I wasn't headin' for your chamber; I was climbing to the one above ye! There lies a real woman, the finest woman in these parts. Oonagh of the ample bosom, Oonagh of the white throat. If yeh weren't so high and mighty ye'd a learnt some Irish and ye'd a known it couldn't possibly be you I would want to lie with. It'd be a poor day for Ireland the day Tadhg O'Flanagain would lie with an English-woman.' The bard rose in indignation from the bed; Isabella trembled for her very life.

'Look at yeh!' he bellowed. 'Yer not a patch on my lovely Oonagh. The cut a yeh there in that wispy bit of a shift, sure there's nothin' there for a man to hold.'

'You're bleeding all over the counterpane; clean yourself up quickly and go!'

'And whose fault is it that I'm bleedin'?' he snarled, and he swung his great legs out on to the floor. Sitting bolt upright on Isabella's bed he addressed her thus:

'I was climbin' up to the Lady Oonagh's chamber, mindin' my own business, thinkin' of all the delights that lay before me, when ye opened the window, a window that's not been opened this forty year. Ye unsettled the ivy that was growin' nicely, and that pulled down wan a Sir Bashel's little gargoyles and it hit me a clatter across the face. 'Twas the luck a God I didn't fall and break me neck.'

*Isabella sat on her bedroom floor; a terrible fit of weeping overcame her. When would this odious man leave? When could she leave this dreadful country and go home? It was all too much for her to bear!*

*The bard looked at her; he smeared his coatsleeve across his bloody face. 'Arra stop,' he said. 'There's no call for ye to be ollagoanin'. Dry yer eyes now there, like a good little girleen; come on sure I didn't mean what I said about yer looks either.' He looked at her disdainfully as she sat shivering on the mat. 'Sure some poor English lad'd like yeh, I'd say.' He handed her a handkerchief. Isabella dried her eyes and the bard pulled back the counterpane.*

*'Where will you go now?' she asked.*

*'Yerra I'll go on up the stairs, sure there's not much Sir Bashel could do to me even if he was able to catch me!'*

*'Why don't you go up the stairs every night?' asked Isabella.*

*'Tis the Lady Oonagh, she prefers her lover scrambling up to her window, facin' all kinds a dangers, and I haven't the heart to disappoint her. She's had it hard, the poor thing, tied to that oul cripple. Now let you get off to sleep; not a word to anyone that yeh saw me and, Miss Isabella, I'm sorry I frightened yeh.'*

Nell yawned and stopped writing; it was nearly ten o'clock but she had made great progress with the Sir Bashel story. I am not writing any more of that, she thought. What's there is more than enough for the next writing class. She decided that her next step would be to type it up neatly and send it out to a publisher, just as a taster. Plenty of contracts were signed between publishers and writers on the strength of a few pages; there was no point in slaving away at it for months if it was likely to be rejected. That done, she could turn her attention to the project nearest her heart: *Brown World*. It was ages since she had touched it. Tomorrow after school, she decided; no point now, it's too late and anyway I'm up to my tonsils in lowbrow fiction: I couldn't rattle up a deep thought tonight to save my life! Bed, she promised herself. She left the table, picking up her new Trollope novels before going up to her bedroom.

# CHAPTER TWELVE

I really ought to turn out the light. I have a very busy day tomorrow, thought Nell, as she lay in bed propped up on four pillows. But *Barchester Towers* was impossible to put down. The shenanigans at the cathedral close at Barchester had gripped her attention, none more so than those of the bishop's wife, Mrs Proudie. She drew her knees up into an inverted 'V' shape, placed her book onto this improvised lectern and thought again of some of the delightful moments in the novel. Trollope was better than Dickens any day, she decided. Or, she corrected herself – remembering received literary wisdom, which said little in favour of Trollope and lots in favour of Dickens – I am enjoying him more. She picked up the book again and turned to the introduction to read some details of his life: his writing was done whilst he held down a full-time and demanding job in the Post Office, a job which also involved extensive travelling. You are useless, she ticked herself off. When did you last write a bit of *Brown World*? Pretending to yourself that you're too busy with teaching to give it the attention it deserves! Fiddling about instead with Sir Bashel and his capers. Sure that's not writing. Trollope, she noted, rose very early and wrote for two hours before his day job claimed his attention. And he wrote in longhand. You're a disgrace!

Nell flattened her pillows and reached for the alarm clock; she set it for six o'clock and lay down to sleep. But sleep would not come; she was tired but her mind was alert. I have done enough Sir Bashel, she thought. He's off to the publishers when he's typed up. These early-morning writing sessions are strictly for *Brown World*. Beginning tomorrow, you write nothing but quality fiction. But what if I can't? she wondered. What if I am so tired at school that I stagger around the place and yawn my way through all the classes? 'Go to bed early,' she answered herself. And what about my social life? Going to bed at half-past nine is hardly conducive to maintaining a social life. 'Be focused,' a little voice in her head told her. This means more to you than hours on the phone chatting mindlessly to friends. You may have something to add to the literary canon! Why else would you be feeling all these urges to write if you didn't? You'll never know if you don't give it a fair shot. She burrowed down into the duvet; she felt snug and warm and happy. A writer, she thought, imagine that! A real writer! Maybe even a good one! Her eyelids finally drooped and Nell dropped off to sleep.

*

Nell shivered in her little boxroom as she sat at her desk. Maybe I should go down to the kitchen. That bloomin' radiator must be on the blink, she thought, as she ran her fingers across it for the third time. Her *Brown World* notebook was on the desk, open at a new page, but there wasn't a word written yet and it was almost six-thirty. No! I am staying here. All my Sir Bashel work has been written at the kitchen table. There are bad creative vibes down there. Stay here, stop moaning and get to work. If you don't smarten yourself it will be time to change out of the tracksuit bottoms and sweatshirt and get ready for school!

*My plan to keep a notebook wasn't working well. I could make no sense of these panic attacks; my description of the day's happenings was incoherent nonesense. Perhaps if I drew some pictures, that would help. I doodled for a moment but that wasn't much better. All that came out were houses and flowers, the things I had drawn as a child. They didn't come anywhere close to capturing the terror I was feeling. I tore the page of drawings out of my notebook. If I ever showed the notebook of this terrible period in my life to anyone, I didn't want those innocuous things there. What I was feeling needed drawings like the Munch drawing.* The Cry, *that was the one. Unless I could represent my anxiety in visual terms like that there wasn't much point in drawing at all. Prose would have to narrate the landscapes of my dread. But I wasn't much of a writer; years and years of mindless memo-writing had killed off whatever natural flair I might have had for creative expression. So, reader, you will have to bear with my somewhat functional prose.*

*I got up from my writing table and paced the apartment. I couldn't settle to writing; watching television was impossible too . I went to the window. It was still light outside, a beautiful June evening. I needed to keep on the move in case my demons assailed me again. I left the apartment, went to my car space and drove to Dun Laoghaire.*

Well, it's a few paragraphs anyway, I'll say that much for it, thought Nell. I can't expect miracles at once. She read it over again in its entirety: God it's awful, isn't it? Nobody with a glimmer of good literary sense could find anything in that. It was half-past seven – time to get ready for school. I'll leave it as it is, come back to it after school and fillet out the dreadful bits. Nell crossed the landing, lifting her sweatshirt over her head as she moved. In the bedroom the radio was playing: 'And, Minister,' David Hanley's voice was saying, 'you did, did you not . . . ' Nell went into the bathroom and scrubbed herself for school.

\*

'Of course there's more Shelley and Keats,' said Nell to Kate. 'There are just no more of their poems in the book. That's the end of their prescribed work for your exam. If you want to read more you'll have to go to the library.'

'So who is next?' asked Emma, consulting the contents page, where she had all the prescribed poems highlighted in Day-Glo pink.

'You won't find what I am going to do today there, Emma,' said Nell. 'I am going to do something different; it's not on the course; that's why I have run off these sheets. Pass them around please, Cliona. If this doesn't work we will go on tomorrow with something from the book, but if you do enjoy it we will spend two, maybe three, classes at it.' Cliona sat down. 'Ready?' asked Nell. 'Now, you don't need to write a thing; just listen. Do not even look at your sheets. I didn't do a sheet for myself because I have a book of this poet's poetry. Nell reached into her school bag and placed a small pile of poetry books on the desk. 'Look at them,' she said. Tell me what you can see.'

There was silence. 'Come on,' said Nell, 'I don't care how silly you think it is, say something.'

'Books, Miss.'

'Fine.'

'Poetry books, Miss Hynes.'

'OK.'

'Big books and small books, Miss Hynes.'

'Yes, now look at them again. They are all different colours but they still have something in common. What is it?'

'Go on, Miss Hynes, tell us,' said Cliona. 'The class will be over soon and we still won't have guessed it.'

'That's you lot all over,' laughed Nell. 'Want the teachers to do all your thinking for you. I'll pass them around; take a good look. You'll kick yourselves if I tell you, because it's staring you straight in the face.'

'Is it to do with the poems?'

'No,' said Nell. 'Have a bit of sense, Jackie. Do you think I would come in here with a bundle of poetry books you had never seen before, expect you to take a glance at them and tell me about them in under five minutes?'

'You might if you were in a mood,' said Jackie, in a huff.

'Well, I'm not in a mood,' said Nell. 'Although, hang on a minute, maybe I am. Look out at that sky. Look at that awful colour; not a bit of blue, not a trace of a cloud. November, dreary, dreary November, the month of the holy souls, too early to think of Christmas!'

'Oh, Miss Hynes, don't remind us; it's ages to the holidays,' sighed Sorcha, and she collapsed into her arms on the table top.

'And these poems are supposed to cheer us up?' asked Kate from the back, very cynically.

'Far be it from me, Miss Sexton, to dispel an adolescent's gloom. Many years in the classroom have shown me what a deep bond there is between an adolescent and her gloom!'

'Miss Hynes, is it the check pattern on the cover?' asked Sinéad.

'Oh, now we've heard everything; the check pattern on the covers!'

'Actually, she's right. Well, right about the covers in any case. Though they're not really check. Look closer and tell me what you see.'

'All the dark squares are letters; each black square is two 'f's,' said Ciara.

'So?' said Kate.

'So,' said Nell, 'printed there before you on all these books is the name of one of the most important publishing houses in England – the two 'fs' stand for Faber and Faber. They have published every major poet you could think of.'

'Which book did you take the photocopied poem from?' asked Cliona.

'Cliona, you had the honour of handing out a poem from that book. Rachel, pass it back to me please.' Rachel slid a thick navy volume across the desk to Nell: Sylvia Plath's *Collected Poems*. 'Never heard of her,' said Sorcha.

'Oh, but you did,' said Nell:

Since Christmas they have lived with us,
Guileless and clear . . .

'Balloons,' Kate, Cliona and Sorcha called out together.

'Exactly, and the rest of you should remember it too. It was in the Junior Cert book. Now let's move on to "Black Rook in Rainy Weather" by Sylvia Plath. 'Your homework for tonight is to read the poem over several times; keep reading it until you can make something of it. I don't mind how small that something is.'

'There's nothing cheerful about this, Miss Hynes,' said Kate, ceasing the battle against a tiny bit of interest which insisted on bubbling up.

'Did I say it would be a cheerful poem?' asked Nell, turning to the class.

'No,' said Jackie. 'But when you said all about the weather and Christmas being ages away, I thought that this might be meant to brighten things up a bit.'

'On the contrary. I might have chosen to read it on a horrible November day because that's exactly the sort of day it was when the rook in the poem was sitting in the tree.'

'Sufferin' Jesus,' whispered Caroline into the heel of her fist.

'I heard that, Caroline,' said Nell.

'Sorry, Miss,' said Caroline, flushing.

The bell rang. 'Is it clear what I want for tomorrow?' A few heads nodded and Nell went out the door to her next class.

*

Nell put her key in the hall door and went into her house. Her energy had flagged seriously that afternoon at school but she was determined to keep to her new regime of rising early to write. Editing was all she intended to do that afternoon: any further serious creation would have to wait until the next morning. She poured herself a glass of sparkling water and went up to her little study. 'Yeuch,' she said, as she finished reading. 'Yeuch and double yeuch,' and she leaned back in her chair to take a good long stretch. Most of that'll have to go, she thought, and she set to with her pen, crossing out large chunks of her ugly prose. She scribbled little notes for herself in the margin; her brain could be very fuddled at six o'clock in the morning. 'Keep her in Dun Laoghaire,' she wrote. 'Juxtapose Dun Laoghaire's beauty on a June evening with her inner turmoil . . . ' Those small aides-mémoires will get me off to a good start in the morning. And, though Nell felt she could get on to a writing roll at that very moment, she fought the urge to keep going. No, she counselled herself. Get stuck in now and you will not go to bed early. You'll be too tired to get up at six tomorrow; your new regime will have collapsed after less than a day. Discipline; that's the key to success; all the great writers say that. Talent is only a small part of it.

Nell stood at the kitchen counter chopping vegetables. The radio was playing: 'A new entry this week,' said a man's voice, 'in paperback fiction. In fourth place is *His Majesty's Courtesan*.' That could be Sir Bashel and myself a few months down the road, mused Nell, as she scooped vegetable parings into her pedal bin. The hot olive oil sizzled in the pan as she dropped all the vegetables into it. She secured the lid tightly and the sound of the vegetables grew muffled. Nell poured herself another glass of sparkling water and sat down.

But could you cope, Nell? said the snobby secondary-school teacher's little voice in her head. Cope with what? another voice in her head rejoined, entering the spirit of the imagined dialogue. With the crass vulgarity of being a successful author of a bestseller. Indeed and I could, and Nell smiled. There was a time when I thought I couldn't, but now I am sure I could. To hell with penury and obscurity. Although I promise I wouldn't make a very ostentatious display of my wealth and I swear I'd never wear pink all the time like Barbara Cartland!

Nell lifted the lid from her pan; the vegetables had shrunk but they still were not ready. She sat down again. And anyway, if Sir Bashel is a rip-roaring success, I am not going to shy away from it. As Heather Connolly said, it was a wonderful achievement within its own limits.

Nell went to the dresser and picked up her little pad of Post-It notes. 'Own your own thrash!!!' she wrote in gigantic letters. She stuck the note to the fridge and laughed. There isn't a soul I would show that to, she thought. Sir Bashel's mine and I am proud of him, she decided. And when they're interviewing me about him and attempting to pigeon-hole me as a novelist with nothing to say, I will retort, 'Well who says just because it's accessible and sells that it couldn't possibly be art? Entertainment is a valid criterion too, you know, and I'm sick of all those anally retentive, opining critics who haven't a creative bone in their bodies; those wouldn't-put-pen-to-paper types unless they could guarantee that it would come out straight away like *Finnegan's Wake*. Oh yes, that's what I'll do. And, thought Nell, sure I always have *Brown World* as my insurance policy!

Hope that doesn't keep me awake, thought Nell, as she drained the last drops of her after-dinner cup of coffee. She got up, cleared the table and washed the dishes. It was just seven o'clock but she didn't want to watch television: something tempting might cause her to waver in her decision to go to bed early. I know what I'll do, she thought, and she went to the space under the stairs where she kept her ancient typewriter. I'll begin to type this up. There were already some pages from the Sir Bashel story on typed pages but the ream of paper she had used was poor quality. She had brought those pages to the writing class and they were the same pages she had given to her mother and Patsy to read: they looked thumbed and shabby now. She would begin afresh on good pages.

Five freshly typed pages lay on the table beside Nell. She was packing up the typewriter. Five more tomorrow and the next day and by the weekend I'll be laughing.

But she didn't want to go to bed just yet. She opened her notebook at a blank page. 'Dear sirs,' she wrote, 'The enclosed pages are a sample of a piece of fiction I am working on at the moment . . . ' No harm to begin drafting the covering letter she would send with Sir Bashel. Brief and to the point, that would be best. Courteous without being obsequious and confident but not obnoxious. 'I realise, sirs, that you receive many unsolicited manuscripts. I should, however, be very appreciative if you could read the enclosed and let me know if something could be done with it.' Or words to that effect, thought Nell, as she re-read the note. Won't type it, though, until all the pages are done. Taking another Post-It note, she scribbled, 'Buy big brown envelopes and stamps.' She went out to her car and stuck the note to the dashboard. One more little job, she thought, and then off to bed. She went to the phone and took it off the hook; it'd be just the night that everybody I know would decide to ring, she thought.

*

Nell groaned as she swung her legs out of bed. She thought the second rising at six o'clock would be easier. But it was worse. She was sorely tempted to reset the clock and get back into bed. But instead she dragged on socks and tracksuit bottoms. This is uncivilised, she thought, as she pulled the bedroom blind up and took a peep outside. All the houses were in complete blackness. An ambulance nee-nawed out on the main road and then there was silence. There was not even the sound of the first buses from the garage labouring their way out to Tallaght as she went to brush her teeth and have her breakfast.

*I decided not to walk on the East Pier. It was too crowded. I crossed the railway bridge and started to go along the West Pier. There were many people out walking but nothing like the numbers of people who frequented the East Pier. I could see them even from where I was standing. It was a beautiful night; yachts and small sailboats bobbed in the harbour and their masts clinked gently in the light evening breeze. The sun was setting. I was nearly halfway down the pier. I looked over my shoulder, back towards Dun Laoghaire. The sunlight glistened on the church spires, which looked like enormous darning needles one might raise to the light to ease a piece of thread through. The ferry had already negotiated its way deftly through the mouth of the harbour and was just a speck on the horizon as I reached the end of the pier. I stood there for a few moments. Young boys and their fathers were fishing from the end of the pier; dogs romped with family parties and children played. Life teemed about me, yet I was alone, so, so alone. The oldest cliché in the book: feeling alone in a crowd. I thought of all the merry people on board the disappearing ferry. Their annual holidays were just beginning. What a contrast they made to all the Irish exiles who had left from this same harbour so many years ago. I thought of Joyce too, an artist going into exile. But he at least had his talent. I had to stay here and I had nothing, and all I had felt today had shown me that I was in a kind of exile too and I did not have a clue when that sensation would leave me for good.*

That's that until I edit it this evening, thought Nell, as she flicked off her desk lamp. She closed the bedroom door and pulled off her writing clothes, dropping them on the landing as she walked into the bathroom and stepped into the shower.

*

'Wonderful, Nell, wonderful,' said Mrs Moran.

'Thanks, Peggy. It was rough at the edges, but they did really well.' First years passed to and fro behind the stage curtains, slipping out of their costumes and back into school uniforms as they walked. Nell and Mrs Moran ducked out of their way.

'Are you sure, Nell, that you won't reconsider putting it on again in the evening for the parents? I don't mean right away but say maybe in a fortnight's time?'

'Miss Hynes, what are we to do with the tankards?' asked Lisa.

'The glasses belong to me,' said Nell. 'Take the tinfoil off, throw it away and put the glasses into that box and leave it in the boot of my car,' said Nell, handing Lisa the keys. 'Take Rachel with you and don't run.'

'Peggy, I appreciate your compliments, but it's too raw, and another two weeks will not make it into the kind of production I would be happy to put on at night.' Don't give in to her, you have enough to do besides traipsing up here in the evenings to rehearsals, thought Nell.

'It seems a shame that only first and second years saw it after all the work you and Olivia have done,' said Mrs Moran. 'And I know the children would love to do it again.'

No doubt you have canvassed their support for this, thought Nell. Well, Peggy, it won't work.

'Those I asked said they would love it,' said Mrs Moran.

'No, Peggy,' said Nell. 'My mind's made up; no can do.'

'I would give you every support. There would be no

problem getting the hall,' said she, whipping out her diary as she spoke. 'Now, let's see. Unislim has it on Tuesdays and the whist people have it on Wednesdays, but other than those nights I can't see a problem . . . ' She looked at Nell expectantly and smiled broadly.

'No, Peggy. I do not have the time. The kids have derived all the benefit I wanted them to have from it already, and I don't have the time.'

'But all that creativity going to waste, Nell. I could really see your hand on the production, could see all you had learned from your drama course.'

And flattery won't work either, Peggy Moran. Who does she think I am? A twenty something trying to keep her sweet?

Olivia appeared through the curtains from the body of the hall. 'That's the last of the bottles and candles, Nell,' she said, heaving a large box on to a table as she spoke. 'Went off well, didn't it? But Jesus, Mary and Joseph, I nearly died when Sir John singed his beard in the candle flame! Oh! Hiya, Peggy, didn't see you there.'

Nell shot Olivia a 'do not let me down now' look as Peggy turned to her.

'Congratulations, Olivia. A wonderful morning's work. Now, I wonder can I enlist your help? I am trying to prevail on Nell to put it on again for a few nights for parents, but so far my requests have fallen on deaf ears.'

'Nights, Peggy, are out of the question. I have a Communion and Confirmation coming up. I am in the church every night for the forseeable future, or at least that's the way it seems.' Olivia looked at Nell and winked. 'We couldn't anyway, Peggy, because of all the phone calls.'

'I'm not with you, Olivia. Phone calls?'

'I thought we told you, but we have been that busy

sure it must have slipped our minds. Peggy, some parents rang in to ask when the real work would be beginning again. They think this is all a waste of time.'

Nice one, Olivia! thought Nell. That'll see her off.

'Oh well, that puts a different complexion on things,' said Mrs Moran, 'They're philistines, of course,' she added hastily. 'Imagine not wanting a rounded education for their daughters,' she threw in for good measure. 'Still, though, we have to put ourselves in their shoes,' she said, and her voice trailed off.

And now let's see her off good and proper, thought Nell. 'Peggy, don't forget that in two weeks the first years will have a student teacher; the parents will think that those weeks are wasted without drawing their fire on top of us over a play.'

'Oh well, that clinches it,' said Mrs Moran. 'Such a shame, though,' and she went off about her business.

'Jehnowah?' said Olivia.

'What?' asked Nell, doubling with laughter.

'We make a great team,' she said. 'Sir John,' she called to Lisa, who was leaving the hall. 'I know you have lived with your fat tummy for weeks now, but the play is over. You are not to wear it to class.'

'Ah, Miss, it's only a bit of a mess,' she said.

'If Mrs Moran got wind of the word that there was messing in classes because of the play she would ban all plays forever and ever and she would be right. Anyway it's Miss Hynes's best cushion and she's had nothing to sit on for weeks. Now scat!'

*

'Miss Hynes to the telephone please, telephone call for Miss Hynes,' the secretary's voice called over the PA system. Now that's all I need, thought Nell. She was sitting in a small office down in the bowels of the school. She was flying through a bundle of corrections, determined not to bring them home. She wanted all her time for typing up Sir Bashel.

'Miss Hynes to the telephone,' insisted the secretary. Nell walked to the office door. 'It's your mother,' the secretary said, as Nell picked up the phone.

'Mammy,' she said. 'Is there anything wrong?'

'Nell, that's rich, you asking me is there anything wrong when I'm demented with worry about you!'

'What are you talking about?'

'I rang you Tuesday night. Your phone was engaged. Rang later and it was still engaged. Nell, I kept ringing until midnight. Then I began to get worried. I tried Patsy to see if she was talking to you, but she couldn't get through to you either . . . '

'Mammy, listen . . . '

'No, Nell, I will not listen. I am not finished. I tried your number on Wednesday morning, still no joy . . . '

'Look, I have a class in three minutes . . . '

'I don't care what you have in three minutes, Nell Hynes. Do you have any idea of the worry you caused me . . . '

Nell pulled the earpiece away from her ear, but she could still hear her mother in full flight:

'Then I thought to myself, she's dead, lying beside the phone; she's had a heart attack or something, was trying to ring the doctor but didn't make it and pulled the phone . . . '

Nell put the phone to her ear again. 'Now you're being

ridiculous, Mammy. I just wanted a couple of early nights. I took the phone off the hook, but I forgot to put it back again. That could happen to anyone. There's no need for all this drama.'

'Drama! That's a nice way to dismiss a mother's care. You know I am not getting any younger. I can't take shocks like that. Do you know that I wanted to jump into the car and go over and see were you all right, only Patsy stopped me!'

'Well, you would have ruined my early night if you had come banging on the door at midnight.'

'Not midnight, Nell, seven in the morning . . . '

'Now, Mammy, that's really over the top . . . '

'It's never over the top to care, when I think . . . '

'Sorry, Mammy, someone needs this line and there's the bell. Have to go, talk to you at the weekend, bye.'

\*

'So, girls, how did you get along with the black book?' Nell asked the fifth years. 'I hope that just because it's last class that I am not going to be greeted with blank faces, yawns and people giving sly looks at their watches. Now, who's going to begin?' There wasn't a sound in the room. All the students looked at their pages, hoping not to catch Nell's eye. Some of them, Nell knew, were just looking at the poem for the first time. 'I haven't a clue what this poem is about, Miss Hynes,' said Laura, 'and I did read it, honest.'

'I don't expect you to know "what it's about", Laura,' said Nell. 'I don't know "what it's about" myself. I think I might have an idea what the poet is getting at, that's all. Now let's approach it very simply first. What is she describing for us?'

'It's a wet miserable day and there's a big black rook sitting on a branch. That much I got and then I got lost, Miss Hynes,' sighed Linda.

'That was a big help, Linda,' laughed Aoife. 'That's only the first verse.'

'Yes, but it does set the scene,' said Nell. 'Just think about that little piece for a moment. What kind of atmosphere is set for us?'

'Gloomy, Miss.'

'Mmmmm, and?'

'She says the leaves are "spotted leaves" so it's a wet autumn day, maybe. That's not a cheerful atmosphere; everything is dying,' offered Tanya,

'Good,' said Nell. 'Now keep going.'

'Can't, Miss,' said Debbie as Nell moved along the row.

'Anyone ever seen a rook?' asked Nell.

'No,' some voices answered.

'Well, I have never seen one, but she does tell us a rook is black,' said Barbara.

'Girls,' said Nell, 'you have all seen rooks; they're members of the crow family and there's plenty of them in the school grounds.'

'I don't know why she wants to put a bird like that in her poem,' said Gillian impatiently. 'Big ugly things; it's not as if they could sing or anything, say like the nightingale.'

'You're on to something there, Gillian,' said Nell. 'Come on now to the next lines:

I do not expect a miracle
Or an accident
To set the sight on fire
In my eye . . .'

'Does she mean that if you were out on a wet day and all you could see was a big ugly rook and his feathers were all droopy and wet, that you wouldn't be expecting to see anything really great?' asked Cliona.

'Exactly,' replied Nell.

'Yeh,' said Cliona. 'But I am still stuck. I don't understand the next bit.'

'"Desultory?"' said Nell. 'Anyone look it up?' Nobody had. 'Look, you all have dictionaries. Look them up when you meet some word you don't know.'

'But Miss Hynes, I always look up words when I don't understand, but then I forget them straight away,' pleaded Jackie.

'Pencil it in in the text,' said Nell. 'We all had to do it in our time. Nobody is born knowing the meaning of every word. "Desultory", according to the dictionary, means, "going constantly from one subject to another, disconnected, unmethodical." Like some of your essays!'

'But that's no help,' whinged Jackie. 'I still don't get "desultory weather", that doesn't make sense.'

Nell looked around the room; there were still several students who hadn't said anything. Kate, Sorcha and Clodagh sat in silence; Sorcha had a multicoloured border drawn on her photocopied page.

'Kate,' asked Nell, 'any ideas?'

'I think she means that the weather is constantly shifting and that she sees no significance in it. It's just the same old round of predictable weathers. Nothing ever happens to set the scene on fire.'

'And?' said Nell.

'So she says let the leaves fall, let the rain fall, it is all meaningless,' finished Kate wearily, almost out-Plathing Plath.

'Well done,' said Nell. 'Now keep reading. Does anything ever happen to relieve all this drabness. Does anything ever "set the sight on fire?"'

'Aah, now I get it,' said Cliona, 'I think I do. Miss Hynes, see the lines about the chair and the table?'

'I do, but read them aloud for us,' said Nell.

'A certain minor light may still
Lean incandescent
Out of kitchen table or chair . . .

'Even though everything is very dreary, sometimes things can look really beautiful and take us by surprise. Do you know what I mean?'

'Yes,' said Nell. 'Atta girl, what kind of things can look beautiful? Does she have to be in what might be conventionally regarded as a beauty spot?'

'No, it might just be the way the light shines on a kitchen chair,' said Emma.

'Miss Hynes, what's "incandescent?"' asked Gillian.

'Anybody know?' asked Nell.

'Shining very very brightly, a white light,' said Sorcha.

'Miss O'Connell,' said Nell, 'I am quite in awe of your versatility.' Sorcha blinked. 'A contribution to the class none but the most unreasonable could quarrel with, whilst expressing yourself visually.'

'But I was listening, Miss Hynes.'

'I know you were. Didn't you just explain "incandescent" for us? And therein lies my awe!'

'Will we be able to use any of this in our exams?' asked Emma.

'Certainly,' lied Nell. 'Surest way to get an 'A' in an essay is to show that you have read extensively. If you have read outside the course and can draw it in intelligently well, you're home and dry.'

'Yeah, Miss, that's if we get an essay on rooks, rain and tables and chairs,' laughed Jackie.

'Jackie's laughing, but she has made a very intelligent point.'

'Me, Miss? I hate this poem, don't understand a word of it. I wish you'd go back to Yeats and Kavanagh and all them.'

'We have just a few minutes left. In a moment I will tell you why I consider Jackie's remark to be a flash of brilliance. For your work for tomorrow I want you to read the poem over and over again. I want you to go as far as "inconsequent." I want you to pay particular attention to the lines:

Out of kitchen table or chair
As if a celestial burning took
Possession of the most obtuse objects
                          now and then –
Thus hallowing an interval
Otherwise inconsequent . . .

'Quick, Miss Hynes, the bell's going to go, why am I brilliant?'

'Girls, when Jackie said she could refer to this poem only if she were asked to write about chairs, tables, rooks and so forth, did you understand her to mean that this poem was *about* those things? I know I did.' Some heads nodded. Nell doubted they were listening at this stage. They just nodded like robots, hoping it would bring her to a speedy conclusion.

'If that's true, then picture this: I am an alien. Nice

little alien minding my own business, darting about in my little flying saucer. And then one day disaster strikes! I run out of my special alien fuel and have to make an emergency stop. Now the really bad news is I have to make my emergency stop out there on that hockey pitch. You earthlings approach, I am terrified, I have never seen such bizarre-looking creatures in all my life!'

'Thanks a bunch, Miss Hynes,' sniffed Orla.

'Serves you right sending Mrs Moran out to ask the alien her business,' said Lisa.

'Now, Lisa, there's no call to be rude,' said Nell. 'We can be rude about you but you can't be rude about us, only in private! So anyway, I send Lisa out to ask the alien what she wants on our hockey pitch, but the poor little thing hasn't a clue what Lisa is talking about. It's raining, you see. The rooks are cawing high up in their trees. Lisa describes all this to the little alien, trying to be friendly, you know. She brings her into the school and sits her at a table and runs off to get Mrs Moran. By this time the poor little thing is babbling earthspeak. "Rooks, rain, tables and chairs" she says over and over. "Explain please, rooks, rain, tables and chairs . . ." Now girls, would you hand her your photocopied sheet of that poem? You would if you agree with Jackie that it's about those things.'

'All right, Miss Hynes, you've made your point,' said Jackie. 'It's not about that. Just don't expect me to come up with the answer, though.'

'I expect all of you to make a very real effort to work out what she is saying,' said Nell. With that, the bell rang and Nell left the class.

# CHAPTER THIRTEEN

At six o'clock on Friday morning Nell sat on the edge of her bed dragging big woolly socks over her frozen feet. There's no way I'm doing this early-morning thing over the weekend as well, she decided. No, I am definitely due a lie-in. I'll just finish typing Sir Bashel and begin to get *Brown World* ready for the off and that can be done at any time. She pulled on her tracksuit bottoms, eased her sweatshirt over her head and went to the kitchen for a quick breakfast. The central heating whooshed into life as she flicked the boiler switch to on. The kettle was humming and as Nell waited for it to come to the boil she filled the washing machine. The wash would be finished when the writing session was over and with luck she might even get to hang the clothes out before she went to school. I need some ancillary staff, she thought, as she filled the ball with liquid. And she smiled. Some day, in the not-very-distant future, I might be recalling the difficulties of the creative woman artist who balances clothes-washing with the complexities of the modern novel. She could almost picture the scene: herself in a television studio, a few good novels already under her belt. How she would hold forth:

'Oh! Indeed it is the late nineties,' she would say, to Jeremy, or Mark or whoever, for this would be London, not Dublin. 'You are quite right; so much has changed for women writers – and changed for the better – since

Jane Austen's day. Of course I have never had to write in the parlour and hide it under my blotter when someone came in. And, to coin a phrase, I have a room of my own, and I was never barred from higher education by virtue of my gender. But it's still not easy for women writers. Women writers only set to creating after the clothes are washed, after the shopping and ironing are done. Jeremy, even those unencumbered by children do not find the path to creativity easy . . . '

The sky above Nell's garden shed was streaking with early morning light. Come on, she said to herself, get your act together, you can daydream tomorrow. She pushed the cereal bowl away from her, picked up her coffee cup and went up to her boxroom.

*It was dark when I left the pier and went back to my car. I got in and began to drive to Rathmines. I felt better. My eyes were heavy with sleep from the sea air. It had certainly been a good idea to come out to Dun Laoghaire. The car ate up the miles and I drove confidently through Blackrock and on into Ballsbridge. I cut down by Herbert Park into Donnybrook and drove across to Rathmines via Appian Way. I felt at ease for the first time in that very long day. All the terrors I had felt that morning in Bewley's and walking through the streets in town had apparently vanished. I hoped and prayed an agnostic's prayer that my terrors were gone for good. As I reached Rathmines I had to drive very slowly – some of the smaller residential streets had been ramped. I came down into second gear and slowed to a snail's pace. And then I saw it: someone behind me was flashing me! Why? I wondered. I wasn't doing anything unusual; my lights were on; I wasn't speeding. I looked in my rear-view mirror. It was a big saloon car and the driver was definitely flashing me. I grew fearful.*

*After the day I had spent, my mind inevitably leaped to sinister conclusions. What if it were someone out to get me? Flashing me just to get me to stop; lull me into a false sense of security by acting like a concerned citizen when really their actions were governed by malevolent forces! I tried to ignore the blinding lights. I kept my head down lower than my mirror, hoping to avoid the glare of the lights. But still the driver flashed and I continued to drive, growing more frightened by the minute. What if I kept going to my apartment? What if he drove behind me all the way? Then he would know where I lived. Sweat trickled down my T-shirt; my arms grew tense as my hands clutched the wheel. I decided I would pull over; if it were all just my overheated imagination he could drive on and then I would be safe. If he were some nutcase I would scream at the top of my lungs and someone would surely come to my rescue: after all, Rathmines was a place which throbbed with life almost twenty-four hours a day. I indicated and pulled into the kerb; in two seconds flat a huge Ford Granada drove past me and he was gone! I sat in the car, took deep breaths and then began to cry. Tears gushed forth, and I made no effort to control them. What had all that been about? How had I worked myself up to such a fever pitch of terror and dread as to assume that another motorist, unaware of my existence, was bearing down on me? I was still not sufficiently composed to resume driving; I sat for some moments in the darkness of the car, drying my eyes and blowing my nose. I started the engine, looked out to see if it was safe to pull out and then saw some more flashing headlights – but this time from oncoming traffic. I killed the engine and decided to stay where I was. And then the flashing headlights disappeared; it was as if the street had swallowed the car up! And then they reappeared, only to disappear again in a matter of seconds. Each time the car reappeared it was closer to where I was*

*parked. And then I saw what was happening. There was a
perfectly rational explanation for what I thought was the
flashing: the cars mounted the ramps, drove over them and
then down onto the flat street; on the ramp their lights were
fully and glaringly in view; as they slipped down to street
level they disappeared. This movement had created my
sensation of being flashed at. I almost cried with relief. I
switched on the engine and drove to my apartment. It was a
joy to know that my fears had been groundless. But why oh
why did some silly trick of the light trigger such profound fears
in me? Surely it wasn't right to be seized by such dread. That
was the question that spun round and round in my head as I
stood in the lift on my way up to my apartment.*

\*

'So, girls,' said Nell to the fifth years, 'what did Plath
mean when she said that a celestial burning could hallow
an interval otherwise inconsequent?'

There was no reply. 'Now, I am not going to answer
my own questions as usual. You must have some idea.'

All heads were down, feigning intense scrutiny of the
photocopied pages. There wouldn't be any volunteers. Nell
would have to pick someone.

'Emma, what's an interval?'

'A break, Miss.'

'And what happens to the few minutes of the interval
if it's "hallowed?"'

Jackie was rustling the pages of her dictionary. 'Jackie,
I'll overlook the fact that the dictionary was to be
consulted for homework if you tell us all quickly what
"hallowed" means.'

'To make holy, Miss.'

'Girls, what would this interval have been like if it hadn't been "hallowed?"'

'Inconsequent.'

'Which means, Deborah?'

'Nothing of any importance happening, Miss.'

'Indeed,' said Nell. 'And, girls, what gave the moment some signifigance?'

'The way the light shone,' said Emma.

'And what kind of an observation is that? Is it positive or negative?'

'Positive,' said Cliona. 'The day was dull and miserable; the sky was overcast. All there was to see was this wet, ugly bird up in the tree.'

'And then the light shone,' said Clodagh, 'and suddenly even the kitchen furniture was lit up and looked special.'

'Well done. Now we are really getting somewhere. Now, move away from tables, chairs, rooks and trees and try to apply what she is saying to life. Any ideas what she might be getting at?'

'Life's pretty drab most of the time,' said Sorcha, 'but now and again the drabness is relieved by something special.'

'Very good. Can you show us where she says that in the poem please?'

'I only know that a rook
Ordering its black feathers can so shine
As to seize my senses, haul
My eyelids up . . . '

'Excellent,' said Nell. 'What do the words "haul" and "seize" suggest to you?'

'Dragging and grabbing, Miss.'

'Splendid. Now why do you think that she would say

"haul my eyelids up"? I mean, think of what delicate little pieces of tissue our eyelids are. Isn't that very violent?'

'But we are so deeply immersed in this nothingness,' said Kate, 'we are nearly annihilated by it . . .' and she trailed off.

'No, Kate, go on,' said Nell.

'See where she says "grant a brief respite from fear of total neutrality . . ."'

'Mmmm,' said Nell.

'Most days are neutral, absolutely dull, but she is hoping for something that might happen which could haul her out of all that. Like, she means it would take something as aggressive and violent as "hauling" to pull us out of that.'

'Miss,' said Sorcha, 'does she mean that life is a bit like a play, and it goes along from day to day, but sometimes something beautiful happens and that becomes an interval in the dreariness?'

'Indeed she does.'

'But that's desperate, Miss,' said Cliona.

'Why?'

'Well, an interval is only a few minutes, so we get much more drabness than niceness.'

'Anybody else agree with Cliona?' asked Nell, and she glanced about the room.

'I agree with Cliona that it's desperate, but I also think that the poet is right,' said Sinéad.

'Is it a completely pessimistic poem?'

'Not completely,' said Emma.

'Elaborate on that, Emma.'

'Well, she says "miracles occur", so that means it's not all terrible, but she says much more about "neutrality" than about "celestial burning", so it's both things, but much more pessimistic, I think.'

'Everybody,' said Nell, 'read it again quickly and tell me this: has any interval in the poem been hallowed? Or has the rook shone?'

'No,' some voices replied.

'How do you know?'

'A certain minor light may still
Lean incandescent . . . '

read Sinéad. 'She's only saying that it might happen.'

'And, Miss Hynes, where she says, "for it could happen",' said Sorcha.

'And how can she say that it could happen?'

'Maybe she has experienced something like this before,' said Jackie.

'Precisely,' said Nell.

'But Miss,' said Ciara, 'isn't there just as much of a chance that a miracle will not occur?'

'Indeed,' said Nell. 'That's what gives the poem its richness. Miracles have occurred before. There have been days when just a beam of light reflecting on a chair or a table have left her dizzy with delight. And, of course, she hopes for other intervals like that, especially as the main play isn't always joyful. There's a chance she will have many more moments but there is an equal or even stronger chance that she won't.'

'Miss Hynes,' said Kate.

'Yes.'

'Even if the moments come, it's not enough.'

'What makes you say that, Kate?'

'Because she says that the miracles are just "tricks of radiance", Miss. This fantastic stuff that she's longing for is nothing really.'

'Yes, and Miss Hynes,' added Sorcha, 'the kind of living she's doing while she is waiting for a miracle is just a "content of sorts" which she has patched together.'

'And what does all that say to you?'

'We're doomed,' said Kate. 'There's no point to anything at all.'

'And what about "the long wait for the angel"?' asked Nell. 'Mightn't that suggest some light at the end of the tunnel?'

'Miss, he probably won't come,' said Jackie.

'And Miss, even if he comes he might be a disappointment,' said Clare.

'And tell me this, girls: will we do another poem by Plath tomorrow or have you had enough?'

'Well, if you could find an easier one I wouldn't mind,' said Cliona.

'And what if I can only find difficult, gloomy ones?'

'I don't mind, Miss Hynes. I always expect the worst,' said Sinéad.

'Good God! I am a lady fast advancing into decrepitude and I don't feel like that.'

'What's decrepititude, Miss?'

'Jackie,' said Nell, 'quick before the bell goes look it up, come on, "de-crep-it-tude".'

'"Wasted, worn out, enfeebled with age and infirmities"'

'Now, even someone like that doesn't think the worst. I am shocked that someone young could.'

'But Miss Hynes,' said Kate, 'if you're expecting the worst you're more prepared.'

'And then if the worst doesn't come you can be much happier than if you were really happy and it all disappeared,' Cliona clarified.

I'll have to think about that a bit,' said Nell, as the bell rang for the end of class.

*

Oh, so it's you,' said Mrs Hynes as Nell turned the key in the hall door of her mother's house. 'I heard the door and I thought it might be Patsy.' Mrs Hynes's tone was frosty; she still hadn't forgiven Nell for making light of her histrionics. This was going to be hard work, and Nell was prepared to make some effort but she wasn't prepared to be abject. Mrs Hynes crossed the hall and went to the kitchen and Nell followed her.

'Tea?' she asked Nell.

'That would be lovely, but you sit down and I'll make it.'

Mrs Hynes sat at the kitchen table, clasped her hands in front of her and sat in silence. That was a supreme effort for her. Nell sighed. Families, she thought. They would wear you out. She filled the kettle, plugged it in and began to put out some mugs.

'Not mugs,' said Mrs Hynes. 'Use the teacups.'

'Right so,' said Nell, and she scalded the teapot. 'Look, I'll get them,' said her mother. 'You've been working all day; just make the tea.'

That was promising. Nell sat down and waited for the tea to draw.

'Did you go home first after school?' asked her mother.

'No, sure look at me, all tights and skirts. Couldn't you tell?'

'True enough,' and Nell thought she saw the beginnings of a smile.

'Anything strange?'

184

'Nothing at all.'

'How's school?'

'Boring,' said Nell, 'but at least it's Friday.'

'They seem to keep you busy enough there. A mother can't ring her daughter when she's up the wall but they give you the third degree. And as for the daughter, when she condescends to come to the phone, she just dismisses her mother's anxieties . . . '

'I couldn't talk properly then, Mammy. I wasn't trying to dismiss you. You just can't say anything private on that phone with all the kids in and out . . . ' Things were looking up: maybe she would get away with just clarifying things and not bother to apologise at all. 'I couldn't say that my phone was deliberately off the hook because that would have involved telling you I was up at six every morning for the last few weeks and that's why I need early nights . . . '

'What has you up at that hour of the morning?'

'Writing, Mammy. It's impossible to get anything done in the evening with corrections and cooking and the phone ringing.'

'Do they know that you're writing at school?'

'Only Olivia. Mrs Moran doesn't know, and they certainly don't know in the office, and that's the way I want to keep it.'

'And quite right too. Sure they'd be madly jealous if they knew they had someone gifted on the staff.'

Yesssss, thought Nell, you're home and dry.

'Time enough,' said her mother, warming to her theme, 'time enough to tell them that you're writing something when you have got a big advance and can resign. Will you eat something with your tea? You must be starving.' Mrs Hynes rose from the table and began to put on her apron.

'Mammy, sit down and listen . . . '

'An omelette, maybe? I could easily rustle up one in a few minutes.'

'Later, maybe. Just sit down for a few moments.'

'I will. Just let me freshen that tea, it must be very strong now.'

'The tea is fine, Mammy. Please sit down.'

'You're quite right to say nothing to the people at school,' Mrs Hynes continued. 'When I think of your poor father and that awful Monsignor Flanagan and the time he gave him. Of course it was all your father's fault opening his big mouth, but then again he was always the same. Weren't they all the same those Hynes's? None of them could keep their mouths shut. I am glad to see you have the sense to keep your business private. That must be something you got from me . . . '

Aha, thought Nell, I have her back onside again and I didn't apologise!

'Mammy,' said Nell, 'what are you going on about? Who is Monsignor Flanagan? What's he got to do with what we are talking about?'

'A very great deal,' said Nell's mother, 'and if you have a bit of patience I'll tell you, but don't try and rush me, I hate the way you girls rush me when I am talking. It just spoils a good story.'

'Yes, Mammy, but I wasn't planning on a long visit. I want to get some writing done.'

'Monsignor Flanagan,' said Mrs Hynes very dramatically, 'was a big ignorant yob of a Galway man.'

'Mammy!' said Nell. 'That's an awful thing to say about a whole county.'

'It's not one bit awful. Just because you hop into your car and head west the minute the school is closed doesn't mean to say that they're all lovely in the west. Monsignor Flanagan was the manager of your father's school when we were first married. Now this was all before you children were born. And poor Enda loved writing little stories and he sent some of his stories to *Ireland's Own* . . . '

'Hurry up, Mammy. Get to the point.'

'*Ireland's Own* published them. Now your poor father was thrilled and he told everyone at school. Someone said it to Monsignor Flanagan and didn't the monsignor call over to Enda one day at school and take him aside. He wondered if the writing wasn't "incompatible with his school duties". His very words! I can still hear your poor father's voice saying them over and over again in the kitchen to me when he came home. That man said your father wasn't giving his job his full attention because of the writing. He had always been wondering, he said, why Enda didn't train the hurling team or go around with the plate for the Mass collections and now he could see why: your father had his mind on something else. Told him to give it all up or the implications could be very serious for his future.'

'What did Daddy do?'

'Kept on writing, of course. This time, though, he listened to me and told nobody about it.'

'Did any more stories get published?'

'Yes, but under another name, and sure then Monsignor Flanagan was moved on and your father wrote what he liked and went back to using his own name. Just goes to show you, though, how jealous people are, especially when it comes to talents. And Nell, in your situation, it's even more important to keep your own counsel because that novel of yours is going to be a great success. I can feel it in my bones.'

'Ah, Mammy, don't be silly.'

'I am not being silly. Now, did you get much done since Patsy and I read it?'

'That's what I couldn't explain properly to you on the office phone. I have been slogging away at it every morning and typing it up in the evening and I am going to post it to a publisher this weekend!'

'But you couldn't have finished it already, could you?'

'No, but I have done a few thousand words more and I will send them that, plus what you have read.'

'And can you do that?'

'Do what?'

'Send a novel to a publisher that isn't finished.'

'Oh yes, that's the way it's done today, they often accept a book on the strength of some pages. Sometimes you hear of large advances being paid out, too.'

'God! Isn't that amazing?'

'Not really. Sure I can tell if a child's essay is shite after two lines!'

'Ah, now that's enough of that. You're getting as bad as Patsy.'

'Yes, but you know what I mean.'

'Do you know something, Nell?' asked her mother, and she began to sniffle.

'No, Mammy. What?'

'I don't know what you mean at all, I don't understand a blessed thing any more.' Tears glistened in her mother's eyes and she started to sniffle.

'Ah, Mammy, don't,' said Nell. Tears started to flow down her mother's cheeks and she reached for her handkerchief.

'What's wrong, Mammy?'

'It's just when I think of your poor father and all his

little stories and that awful monsignor and all the other awful old canons tormenting those poor teachers . . . '

'I know, Mammy. It was awful.'

Mrs Hynes blew her nose. 'Nell, I am having a little weep because I am happy . . . '

'I don't follow, Mammy.'

'Can't you see? I am happy because things are so different. Look at you and Patsy teaching away, but neither of you goes near a church. And as for Enda over in London, God knows what he gets up to! No canons or monsignors are bossing you around. Your book will get published and you'll make a fortune.' Mrs Hynes dried her eyes.

'Ah well now. I don't know about a fortune . . . '

'Of course you will make a fortune. That Sir Bashel story is wonderful. Now I am going to make us something to eat. You have got time to stay for a bite to eat, haven't you?'

'Yes, all I am doing this evening is some typing.' Her mother got up from the table and went to the fridge. She took out a bowl of eggs. Nell sat thinking. I feel a bit guilty letting her think that all I am working on is Sir Bashel. Still, though, if there ever comes a time when she needs to hear about *Brown World* I will deal with it then, cross that bridge if and when I ever come to it.

'Nell?'

'Yes.'

'An omelette?'

'That would be lovely, Mammy, thanks.'

*

Nell?' said the unfamiliar male voice on the phone on Saturday morning.

'Speaking.'

'Nell, this is Con McDermot, Niall Colleran's friend. We met at *Hedda Gabler*, do you remember?'

'Yes, Con, of course I remember. What can I do for you?'

'I am having some friends round for drinks this evening. I was wondering if you would like to join us. I am very sorry about the short notice. Olivia gave me your number and I have been trying you all week but your phone appears to be on the blink.'

'That's a long story,' laughed Nell.

'Well, can you make it? There'll be lots of people here you know already and it should be very enjoyable.' Nell felt the old knot tightening in her stomach again. And she thought of Hugh and when they had first met. It was a beautiful evening in May. Nell had bumped into Niall Colleran as she was walking to the pub to meet some friends. Hugh and Niall Colleran had been sharing a house. Hugh was tall; his hair was curly and he had the bluest eyes. 'Of course you've never met this madman, Nell,' said Niall, 'sure you haven't?' Nell had been watching him out of the corner of her eye as Niall spoke and what she had only been able to take in with one eye had made her head swirl . . .

Could I go down that road again? What's to say that going for drinks is 'going down that road'? Didn't you tell yourself you were off relationships for ever? Going to devote yourself to writing? But sure you always wanted to write. Even Hugh knew that. In fact wasn't he always saying you should stop talking about it and do it? Why should writing preclude sex? You might be off relationships temporarily, but you shouldn't be off sex! That's not natural!

'Love to. Hang on while I get a pen.' Nell had a pen beside her but he wasn't to know that. Well, she thought, isn't that just what the doctor ordered? Your libido has been on hold while you were creating and just as you're out the door to post the fruits of your labours, he rings. Con, as she recalled, was nice, and even if he turned out to be disappointing you never knew who else might be there too. She was ready to cast her net again, more than ready to reel someone nice in!

'I'm back, Con. Give me the address again,' she said, and she began to scribble. 'That's fine. I look forward to it, bye.'

Nell went to the kitchen. Two fat brown envelopes were lying on the table: *Brown World* and Sir Bashel O'Dell. Both typed up and ready to go. She picked up her jacket and the envelopes, pulled the hall door shut and walked to the letter box.

It was a crisp November morning. The sky, for once, was blue. And there wasn't a rook arranging his wet feathers to be seen! Gerry over the road was washing his car but she avoided him. She wanted to savour this moment in private.

I am Nell Hynes the author, she whispered to herself, hoping her lips were not moving too obviously. I am walking to Rathmines to my lucky postbox to post not one, but two, novels. And then when I come home I am going to have something to eat, shower and change, take endless care dressing and then even greater care to make it all look nothing. And when I am ready I am going out, and by hook or by crook I am going to have some kind of a sexual encounter, preferably casual! After all, I do not want a pimply little PhD student twenty years from now presenting a paper to some symposium entitled: 'Hynes: a study in celibacy and its implications for creative endeavour'!